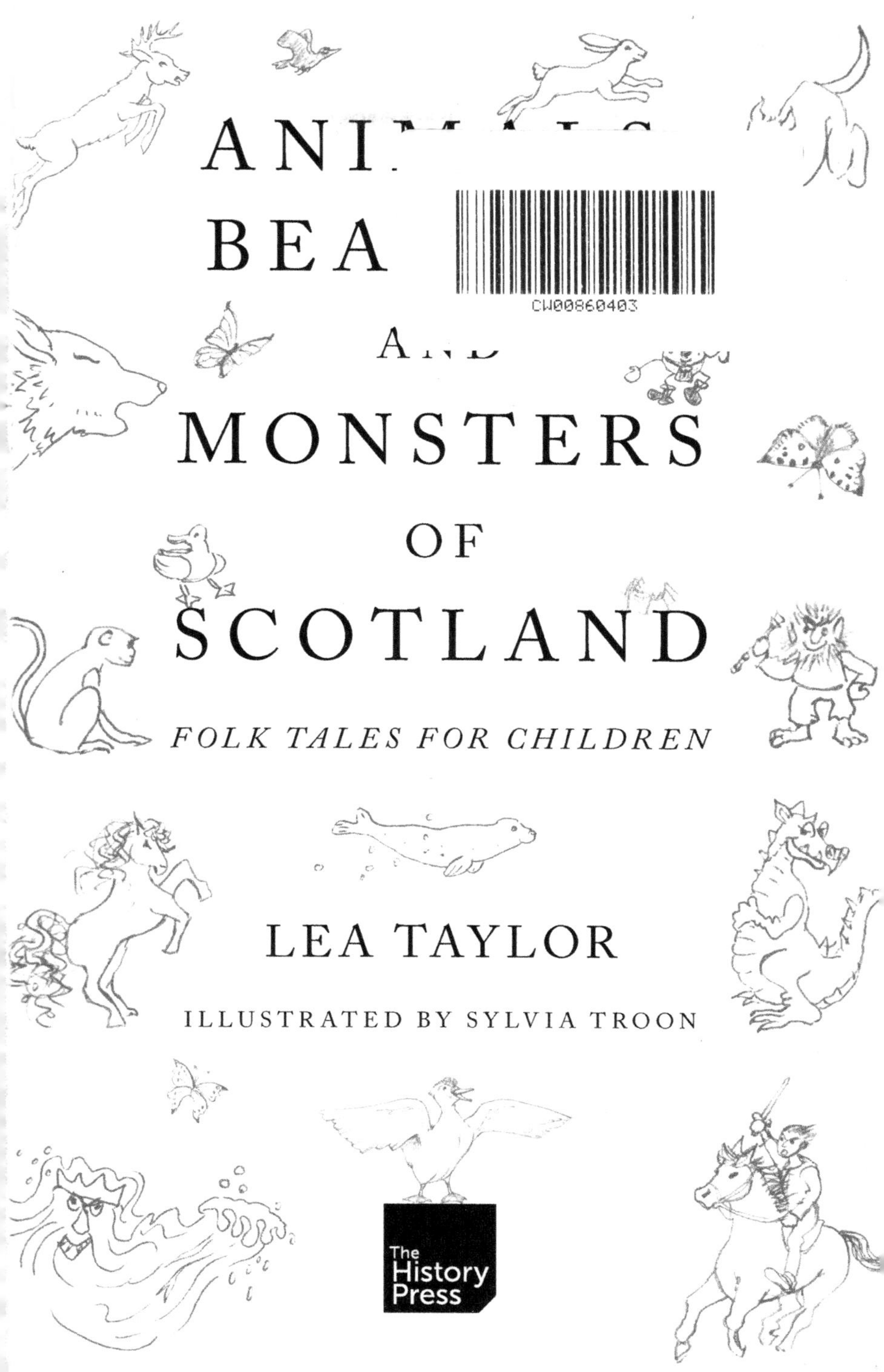

ANI
BEA

A

MONSTERS OF SCOTLAND

FOLK TALES FOR CHILDREN

LEA TAYLOR

ILLUSTRATED BY SYLVIA TROON

The History Press

Dedicated to Andy and Cameron

First published 2019
Reprinted 2019

The History Press
The Mill, Brimscombe Port
Stroud, Gloucestershire, GL5 2QG
www.thehistorypress.co.uk

British Library Cataloguing in Publication Data.
A catalogue record for this book is available from the British Library.

ISBN 978 0 7509 8686 1
Typesetting and origination by The History Press
Printed in Great Britain by TJ International Ltd, Padstow, Cornwall

CONTENTS

ABOUT THE AUTHOR

Lea uses words to make a living. Her main job is through working as a freelance storyteller – this aspect of her work is diverse, ranging from writer/storyteller residencies, to working with schools, government agencies or residential care homes doing reminiscence work. She is no stranger to performance work and has written a number of pieces for festivals and tours. It is very much hoped that you enjoy and share these stories as much as Lea has enjoyed writing them.

ABOUT THE ILLUSTRATOR

Sylvia has found it thoroughly enjoyable to draw the creatures for this book – especially the wee midgies! Since her studies at Edinburgh College of Art she has taught in schools, been a puppeteer and storyteller, and recently created books for Historic Environment Scotland. She is now concentrating on painting, and writing and illustrating her own stories, as well as working with Lea.

INTRODUCTION

In writing this book I have drawn upon folk tales and traditional tales from the length and breadth of Scotland. In some instances I have used elements of well-kept traditional tales and introduced bits of them into the story. Most of the traditional tales are formulaic and so I do not feel I have strayed too far, merely looked at the story with a fresh eye. I have also actively sought to contemporise some of the stories to give them a twenty-first century feel. All stories morph and change in their telling, and this is the reason why I have taken this approach.

I truly hope you enjoy reading this book as much as I have enjoyed researching and writing it.

ACKNOWLEDGEMENTS

Without the assistance of a number of wonderful helpers the task of bringing this book to print would have been a long and onerous one. Thanks to my husband, Andy, for his tireless patience and endless cups of tea. To Cameron for being my story tester and especially to Sylvia Troon for her wise comments, encouragement and endless support. This really has been a wonderful collaboration with lots of surprises along the way.

1

JACK AND THE BLUE MEN OF THE MINCH

Jack was a typical boy. He liked his football, his computer games, his music, especially grime music. A guaranteed wind-up for his mum as she was forever asking him to turn it down or off. When his father died, they moved to the west side of the Isle of Lewis, not far from the Callanish Stones, to be nearer to his mum's family. One afternoon his Uncle Gregor took him out on a special trip in his fishing boat on one of Scotland's roughest stretches of water, the Minch. But before they had a chance to cast their nets a sudden storm blew up and they had to cut the trip short. Life in Lewis was quite a radical departure from what Jack had been used to in the city.

Jack, like all teenagers, was not the most forthcoming of lads when it came to helping around the house. His mother moaned and cajoled him into helping but he never did anything without being asked. The day came when his mother finally broke down and cried, 'Jack, it's no good son. I can't be carrying you anymore. You either pull your weight or you'll have to leave. I simply can't afford to do this any longer.'

Jack was shocked. He hadn't seen this one coming – and to think that his mother was prepared to ask him to leave. It was unthinkable. Hurt and angry, Jack left the house, slamming the door behind him. He needed time to think, to take all that had been put before him in. He walked aimlessly for a long while, not really taking any notice of where he was going or how late it was getting. He was hungry and tired, his feet were sore but he still wasn't ready to go home. Part of him wanted to stay away to make his mother worry, make her feel bad about what she had said, so seeing a large stone that offered a bit of shade, he sat himself down next to it. Its coolness and shape somehow fitted perfectly with his back. He stretched his feet out and tilted his head to feel the gentle breeze on his face, and before he knew it he had fallen fast asleep.

The stone radiated a hum. There was something about it that connected the stone to the land – the very heart of the land that spoke of ancient ancestors – their voices somehow crept into his head and pulled him down into the depths of the earth, down into its very core. Jack felt himself falling, could see images flickering past him. Men with flocks of sheep. People with carts loaded with belongings looking sad and lost. Soldiers on horses carrying flags, soldiers with pikes on foot. Strange large creatures, prehistoric perhaps? Blue faces, bodies with fish scales moving, perhaps swimming powerfully through water. Suddenly he landed in a huge cavernous cave. Its light shone pearlescent and luminous – the whole of the cave was covered in mother of pearl. He hardly had time to take it in when someone or something with great strength lifted him up by the arm and pulled him towards the centre of the room.

A crowd of dark figures stood there, their backs to him, facing inwards. Jack felt himself being pushed towards the centre, stumbling through and past tall, sticky forms. As he brushed past he thought of tough elastic, the kind that pulled at the hairs on his arm. When he broke through the throng he was confronted by a huge octopus dancing an eightsome reel to its appreciative audience. As the music subsided, the bodies stood back, leaving Jack standing out all on his own. All eyes were upon him but in particular those of a huge blue man seated on a seaweed throne before him. The throne was set upon a dais and surrounded by the jawbone of a great shark or huge whale.

The blue man wore a crown made of elaborate seashells and cape patterned with images of starfish, seahorses and fish. In his huge right hand he gripped a sceptre made from what looked like a narwhal's tusk. His grey-blue face was as old and wrinkled as Father Time's. He smiled to reveal teeth, yellow and jagged, like the rows of teeth set in the jawbone around the throne. With a bony blue finger, the chief beckoned Jack to come closer, his eyes, slits of blue against a yellow background, blinked in a rhythmic fashion.

'You tuned in to the pulse of the land. You called the ancient ones,' he murmured, his voice escaping between bursts of bubbles.

'The ancient Storm Kelpies chorused the throng with a rush of oxygen rising upwards.

'Perform your quest or submit yourself to the Kingdom of Blue.' The chief leant forward as if to impress his point.

Jack was perplexed; he wasn't aware of calling anyone. Pulse of the land? Quest? What was this strange man on about? 'Dude, you got me all wrong,' he ventured, but the chief and his subjects remained still, staring at him impassively. Only the seaweed fronds swayed gently in the water.

'Perform!' commanded the chief.

'Yes, perform!' shouted one of the Blue Men, poking him in the back with a stubby finger. The other Blue Men moved in closer. They looked quite menacing.

Jack stood stock still. How he wished he was at home with his mother. He would clean up his room, help around the house, even hoover and chop wood. Anything to be away from here.

'You dare to defy the Blue Men of the Minch? Perform – for your life depends upon it,' said the blue man who had poked him. There followed another pause. 'Very well then.' The blue man nodded at the chief as if taking his cue, 'I will give you your tasks – and should you fail, you will live the rest of your days here as the chief's slave. Now, sing to please the chief!'

Sing! Jack had never sung in public. He wasn't even sure he *could* sing and then his mind went blank. He couldn't think of a single song. Suddenly he was reminded of a small part he played in the school play. There he had stood on the stage, illuminated by the spotlight for all the school, its teachers, children and parents to see and he had forgotten his lines.

'Sing!' commanded the chief, thumping the floor of his throne with his narwhal tusk. 'Sing,' chanted the audience. Whorl patterns appeared in the water, like mini tornadoes. And when the Blue Men became excited it seemed that one whorl pattern joined another and another. As he witnessed this, Jack started to feel himself being drawn in by the vortex they created, his feet lifting off the floor.

Then the chief raised the narwhal tusk and everyone became silent. The whorls slowed and disappeared just as quickly as they had appeared.

At first Jack ventured a nursery rhyme, 'Humpty Dumpty', but even he could tell it wasn't going down well. Then he sang 'Flower of Scotland' with a bit more gusto. The chief grimaced, some put their hands over their ears. After a while a fish swam by and plugged itself into Jack's mouth, at which everyone cheered.

'Now dance!' commanded the chief.

'Dance? You're kidding me!' moaned Jack. 'I cannae dance to save masel.'

The chief thumped the floor with his narwhal tusk and issued the order once more, 'Dance!'

Feeling incredibly self-conscious, Jack began to shuffle his feet this way and that. When he stamped the floor sand rose in the water, creating small foggy clouds. Until that moment he hadn't noticed that he was breathing under water. He made a mental note to himself that dancing under water is not an easy feat.

He began to feel a rhythm, hear its beat inside his head. His feet started to respond. He slipped a moon walk dance move into the routine, a smile appeared on his lips, and he was just thinking 'A'm no so bad at this' when the octopus stretched out a couple of its tentacles and grabbed him by the ankles. Before he knew it, he was face-planted in the sand and all the Blue Men were roaring with laughter. Even the chief was slapping his sides.

Jack got to his feet, quite cross and not a little embarrassed. The Blue Man stepped forward once more and exclaimed, 'This is your last chance to prove yourself and obtain your freedom. The challenge is …'

Jack could feel his heart thumping as if it was trying to free itself from his chest. He thought of those competitions on the telly where they pause a couple of moments before announcing the winner to enhance the suspense.

'In accordance with the dictates of the Blue.'

'The Blue' chanted the rest of the crowd in unison while thumping their chests emphatically.

'We will demand a Storm Kelpie tradition, drawn up by our ancestors who lived in the Minch and swam between what you call Lewis and the Shiant islands many moons before us. In their honour, we call upon a rhyming duel.'

'A rhyming duel,' chanted the crowd, releasing another burst of bubbles.

'Eh? What's that when it's at hame?'

'Precisely what they said,' stated the chief. 'I say a rhyme, then you, then me and so on until whoever fails first.'

'Oh, I see. Well, if that's the case, you go first, efter all you're the chief!'

And so the duelling began. The chief started with a simple rhyme immediately followed by Jack. He surprised himself, his rhyme was quick and snappy. He caught sight of the nodding approval of the onlookers and it made him feel a little bolder. The chief responded with another short rhyme, only to find Jack ready with a witty rejoinder. The duelling continued for almost an hour, by which time the chief was losing momentum. Finally he hesitated and mumbled, he ummed and chewed his lip. His subjects coughed and shifted themselves uncomfortably.

Jack seized his chance. Drawing his shoulders up and standing with his feet hip-width apart, he took in a deep breath and began:

> Oh chief, oh king,
> You can de yer thing
> whit ever yer thing may be
> But am telling you this
> fer a seagulls kiss
> I couldnae gie a fig or a flee
> Ye can keep your sea
> and yer funny blue knees
> coz I'm gonnae tae say it straight
> Ill no be yer slave
> going down to the grave
> Noo I'm off to ma bed coz it's late.

He finished with a flourish, a curt wee bow that was greeted with rapturous applause. Even the chief leapt up from his throne to shake Jack's hand and clap him on the back. Upon which, a small shoal of fish entered the arena and performed a synchronised swimming routine. When they were finished the chief addressed his subjects, exuberantly waving his narwhal tusk.

'Friends, Blue Men, Countrymen. Today we have witnessed a feat never seen before – the out-rhyming of the chief. Our competitor has earned his freedom and his dearest wish to return home to help his mother and clean up his room.'

'Clean up his room,' chorused the Blue Men.

'Hame to clean up ma room,' said Jack.

The chief snapped off a small section from the tip of the narwhal's tusk and presented it ceremoniously to Jack.

'Thank you,' smiled Jack, and in what seemed like a nanosecond, he experienced a weird sensation, like being shuggled at his shoulders and tickled on his toes. Suddenly he found himself wide awake, sitting with his back to the standing stone.

'Hame to clean up ma room?' he laughed aloud in puzzlement. 'That was some dream.' But then he looked down to find he was holding something strange in his hand. As he uncurled his fingers he found that the object was nothing more than the tip of a narwhal's tusk.

2

KELPIE CAPERS

It's a rare thing for kelpies to meet up in groups as generally they are solitary creatures, haunting the lochs and burns around Scotland. But with the advent of the giant kelpie head sculptures in Falkirk and all the fuss it created, things changed, for a short while at least.

When word got out, kelpies near and far agreed that they had to meet to decide what, if anything, needed to be done about it and whom, if anyone, was going to deal with this potential problem. After all we had our reputations to keep, the kelpies' code had to be upheld and all the other things in between needed to be considered.

Gathering the herd together was not an easy thing. Where to meet, and when, proved to be a real sticking point. After all, Kelpies don't use social media, texts, phones or even letters for that matter. Everything had to go out by 'word of muzzle'. And then there's the problem of getting to the appointed place. Kelpies can't exactly use public transport or main roads now can they?

Finally it was agreed that the herd should meet at the Kelpie's Stane, near the River Don in Aberdeen. It's been a popular holiday spot for kelpies Scotland-wide for the last several hundred years at least, so it proved to be a popular choice. The gathering was quite an event; Kelpies reunited, who'd have thought it! It was all rubbery smiles (kelpie selfies), prancing hooves, whinnies of delight and galloping about up and down the River Don in a mindless fashion for a while; until we had galloped the excitement out of ourselves at least. We were one great big herd of black, fit-looking horses complete with customised silver bridles, like Appleby Cross fair without the people.

Naturally one of the first things discussed was who among us had posed for the kelpie structures. The general consensus was that 'Falkirk Shuggie' was responsible, but he was having 'nane o it' and in hindsight he was probably right. His nostrils are far too close together in any case. Personally I would have put my shiny hoof on it being Shona from Invergowrie; she always acted as if she were a cut above everyone else.

The best thing to come out of the gathering, aside from meeting old friends or enemies for that matter, was the stories of the encounters we had had with humans. The lives we had taken and the ones that got away. After all, we're not exactly known for being kind and considerate are we?

The best story of the night to my mind was the one related by 'Lachlan of Loch Leven', Lackie to his neighbours. Late one night, when he was trotting about the loch minding his own business, he happened to notice a faint light near the perimeter. The light stood out in his mind because, like he said, 'It was a faint one coming from inside a canvas construction.' At its entrance he saw two heads peeking out, staring at him.

Lackie couldn't stand being started at, particularly by complete strangers. He said the faces were staring so hard that they didn't notice a small wave of midgies flying towards them. They didn't feel their first initial 'bites'.

Lackie took this as a cue to make his presence known. He liked grand entrances. He hauled himself up and out of the loch and, standing right before the light of the tent, just for effect you understand, put a hoof on the top of the tent frame, coughed and bent down to peer in and give the campers his most malevolent stare.

The male camper was very unimpressed. Frightened? He was raging! He squeezed his large body out of the tent and stood eyeball to eyeball in front of Lachlan. 'What is it?' he spluttered. 'What exactly do you think you're doing to my tent?' He pushed a pudgy finger into Lackie's muzzle. 'Do ye ken how much a decent tent costs?' He looked back at his companion as if for reassurance. She was busy swatting at midgies.

Lackie cocked his head to one side and replied in his rich, deep kelpie baritone, 'You'll no be needin it where you're going …' all the while maintaining a fixed eye contact.

'Aye richt, and where might that be, pal?' The camper looked Lackie squarely in the eye and folded his arms. In the background his girlfriend, still swatting, egged him on, 'That's right Bazzer, you get him telt!'

Lackie merely looked over to the middle of the loch, raised his eyebrows and gave his infamous grin, a sparkle of light glinting off his jagged teeth.

'Ah, point taken.' Mr Camper suddenly realised that he was probably out of his depth and, sounding rather sheepish, ventured, 'Might I ask for one wee thing before we meet our end?' Lackie, still levelling his gaze, raised his eyebrows again. 'I'd like to sing a wee song to ma ancestors.'

A long pause ensued. Somewhere in the middle of the loch a fish jumped, creating a splash. The midgies swarmed off.

'Och very well then, if you really huv to,' answered Lackie with an impatient sigh.

Mr Camper reached into the tent to bring out a bottle of Irn-Bru. 'Ah need to whet ma whistle first,' he said. Then he twisted off the bottle top with a flourish and took himself a big draught, his Adam's apple bouncing up and down with each gulp.

'Ah!' he said, wiping his mouth with the back of his hand . 'Made frae girders that stuff. I hud that in ma bottle when I wiz a wee bairn an it niver did me any hairm. Would ye like a wee nip? It'll keep the cold out – I'll wager its chilly doon there!' Lackie thought for a moment.

'Aye, I don't mind if I do. I've heard o' that Irn-Bru and always wondered what it tasted like.'

The man stepped forward, bottle primed and ready to empty into Lackie's open muzzle. Lackie had a wee chuckle to himself noting camper man's alarm at his sharp teeth, or perhaps it was his bad breath, he couldn't quite decide. Either way, he was rather pleased with the impression he made.

But things soon changed about. Once the drink was poured Lackie claimed the effect was instantaneous. He said it felt like his eyes lit up from the inside, as though he had swallowed a bolt of lightning that pulsed throughout his whole body.

Meanwhile, camper man opened his mouth to sing. He sang such a sad, mournful tune that Lackie, yes big rufty-tufty Lackie, had tears rolling down his cheeks. Greetin like a foal so he was. At this point the woman in the tent joined in.

'Ma shot noo,' she shouted as she scrambled out the tent. She threw her head back and opened her throat to the stars.

Her voice was coarse and tuneless. Each note grated on Lackie's delicate ears. He had never heard anything so bad. He shook his head and squeezed his eyes shut while trying to cover his ears with his hooves. 'Stop, please stop,' he begged. But the singer continued to torture our poor kelpie and probably everything else within earshot.

Tears of pain streaked down Lackie's muzzle. The campers could see that Lackie was beginning to break. His withers trembled, he hung his head, then he turned rapidly and ran, disappearing into the loch's murky depths.

Only when the last ripples on the surface of the water disappeared did the singer finally shut up. The campers looked at each other jubilantly and high-fived. 'Your singing, lass, kills 'em every time!' And as if nothing had happened, they climbed back into their tent and zipped up the entrance.

None of us thought any worse of Lackie after that story. Indeed, we thought him courageous to share his 'not-so-great-ending' story and show his sensitive side. Since then, we've always been wary of campers, particularly the ones who sing!

3

THE GREEDY TROWS OF ORKNEY

There was once an old woman who lived all alone in a wee cottage on Orkney. She had no family but was known and loved by all who lived locally for her tasty bannocks. These were considered to be the best bannocks for miles around.

Now, the old lady was quite poor and so to make ends meet she would cook extra bannocks and sell them to the local shop. It was often the case that the bannocks were sold out within ten minutes. So popular were they that people would hang about and wait to watch her coming down the road with her plate laden with tasty treats.

On this one particular day, she mixed the dough and patted the bannocks into shape and cooked them on the griddle like she always did. But as she put them on the plate she accidentally knocked the plate onto the floor. The bannocks rolled right off the plate, out of the door, and across the road. They kept right on rolling until they stopped at a wee bush. The old lady ran as fast as she could after them.

She was just about to pick them up when a small, hairy hand reached out, picked up the bannocks and disappeared down a hidden hole at the side of the bush. The old lady was so surprised and cross, she followed the hand that had snatched the bannocks down the hole. The hole led to a tunnel that fed into another tunnel that dropped down, down deep into the depths of the earth. Finally she popped out the end of the tunnel with

a thump into to a big wide cave. It was fairly dark and dank. It took her eyes several moments to adjust. When she looked around she could see a sea of strange creatures no taller than her thigh, and she wasn't very tall herself. It was their eyes that she saw first. All round and piggy-like, the whites stood out in the darkness. The creatures were small and hairy with spindly arms and legs, and, on closer examination, had dirty fingernails. She couldn't abide dirty fingernails.

The cave was home to a clan of trows. They stood there, greedily licking and smacking their lips. 'More bannocks,' they cried. Their leader addressed her, 'Who made these wonderful, delicious bannocks?' The old lady was flattered. She straightened her back and said with a smile, 'I am the person who made the bannocks.'

She looked around and saw the trows had stuffed themselves with them. They were burping and pumping and making some very rude noises without apology. She stiffened – she couldn't abide bad manners either. The smile slipped off her face as she remembered that the bannocks the greedy trows had filled their faces with were meant for her tea!

Through gritted teeth she spat, 'Yes, I was the person who took the time and effort to make the bannocks *for my tea* and now I have nothing to eat, you bad-mannered little trows!'

The leader of the trows stepped forward, cleared his throat and said, 'Well, madam, I'm sure we can find a happy solution for this. How about we provide more of the ingredients needed and you can use our kitchen to cook more bannocks so we can all eat to our hearts content.' The old lady was so hungry she could hardly think straight and so she agreed.

The trow leader led her into the kitchen. There he took down a huge pot. 'This,' he said, 'was forged by our trow ancestors at the dawn of time. See how sturdy and light it is.' He lifted it up with his pinkie finger as if it were a feather. Then he washed it in the burn that ran to the side of the kitchen area. Next he placed a teaspoon of oatmeal into the pot with a bit of butter and flour.

'You are pulling my leg aren't you?' said the old lady. 'That wouldn't be enough to feed a mouse, let alone a horde of trows, or myself for that matter.'

The trow leader wrinkled his face in what can only have been something akin to a smile. Then, standing on tippy-toes, he took down from the top shelf an elaborately carved wooden spurtle. It was shaped like a thistle with leaves at the handle and slim at the shaft. He stirred once, twice, three times and suddenly the contents of the pot tripled in size. 'You try,' he offered, handing the spurtle to the old lady. Intrigued, she turned the handle three times and found that the contents had indeed tripled in size again. 'I'll leave you to it,' said the trow leader with a curt little bow, and left the kitchen.

The old lady set to work. Mixing the dough, patting it into bannock shapes and then setting them on to the hot griddle to cook. She made many bannocks and finally took them out to rapturous applause from the hungry trows. No sooner had she set them on the table when scores of little hairy hands reached in and grabbed. They stuffed the bannocks into their greedy mouths, making loud slurping noises and grunts of approval, their sharp teeth chomping furiously. When they had finished they shouted, 'More bannocks, more bannocks!'

reaching with their little spindly trow hands and thumping the table.

So, the old lady set to work again making the dough for the bannocks. She took the pot and washed it in the burn, filled it with a small amount of the ingredients and, taking the special spurtle, stirred the pot a number of times until it had just the right amount to feed the greedy trows. As she worked, mixing and kneading the dough, she wondered how, or if, she was ever going to get free of the trows. They looked like they could eat and eat and eat and keep on eating! But she was a clever old lady, she knew that somehow she would find a way; she would just have to put her thinking cap on.

When making the third batch of bannocks the old lady began to sing a lilting lullaby in her soft reedy voice. After a while she noticed that the trows had become quiet and still. When she looked out at them she noticed that they were all fast asleep, snoring softly as only trows can do. Now, she thought, with a flicker of excitement, now I have the chance to make my getaway, but how and where? The tunnel I fell down is far too steep for my old bones to climb, and I can't swim out of the burn. Then suddenly she stopped and clasped her hands together, she had an idea.

She looked at the large pot and a smile spread across her face. All the while she continued singing and the trows slept on. Then she took the pot down to the burn. She had remembered that land trows (which is what they were), hated water so much that they didn't even like getting their toes wet and they never, ever washed.

Carefully she put the pot in the water, climbed into it and, using the spurtle, cast the strange pot-vessel off into the burn. It travelled slowly in the water, bobbing up and down gently until it reached the middle of the burn, where it began to pick up speed. The little old lady giggled with glee but unfortunately, in her excitement, completely forgot to sing.

One by one, the sleepy trows woke up and, realising that something was wrong, ran to the kitchen. From there they could see the old lady floating downstream in the pot. They crowded along the banks of the burn shouting, 'More bannocks, more bannocks,' with spindly fists raised in the air. But the old lady ignored them and paddled faster with her hands in an effort to put more distance between herself and the angry trows. She thought she was safe, that she had every chance of getting away. However, the trows had other plans. She was not going to get away with this. They dropped to their hairy little knees and began to slurp up the water. The old lady laughed. 'You're ridiculous,' she shouted.

They continued to guzzle noisily. The old lady looked over the side of the pot. Something was definitely happening. The water was going down, and doing so at an alarming rate. She began to paddle faster, sweat appearing on her brow. She looked back at the trows and could see they were visibly expanding, bloating up like little hairy balls with jaggy teeth and eyes like ping-pongs. When the pot began to bump and scrape along the bottom of the burn and fish started jumping into the pot alongside her, the old lady became really worried. She looked at the fish flapping on the bottom of the puddled burn bed and at those in her pot and was miserable. I don't want to live the rest of my life cooking bannocks for ungrateful trows, she thought.

At a loss to know what else to do, and desperate to get away, the old lady picked up the fish and threw them at the guzzling trows. 'Take that, you greedy trows. Stuff your faces with these fish!' she shouted.

To her surprise, the trows opened their mouths to receive the fish and in doing so, all the water they had sucked up gushed out of their mouths back into the burn. The pot lifted as the water level rose. As it started to move, the old lady paddled like her life depended on it and soon she and the pot sailed out of sight. She drifted and paddled along some windy tunnels and finally out into bright daylight. Miraculously, she ended up on a bank at the end of the village near to where she lived. She couldn't believe her luck.

When she got home, tired and bedraggled, she made herself some fine bannocks and sat down to feast, all the while thinking of her strange trow encounter. With the spurtle safely in her possession she decided she would put it to good use and the very next day set about making a huge batch of bannocks to sell. In time she had saved up enough money to open her very own restaurant. Her reputation went before her and after a while people came from far and wide to sample her wares. But every night, after she closed the restaurant, she would always leave a big plate of bannocks for the trows by the bush where she had first encountered them. After all, had it not been for them, she wouldn't be where she was now.

4

THE SPIDER'S TALE

Enough is enough. It's about time you all heard my point of view. After all, if it hadn't been for me, none of the events in history would have happened. I think it's rather disgraceful really that nobody has bothered to get my story. Indeed, my name isn't even mentioned. I'm just 'the spider'.

So, let's start at the very beginning, where all good stories start. My name, well, it doesn't quite translate from spider language to yours, so, in order to make things easy for you, let's just call me Lefty. I was born in the glen, well, when I say born, I actually hatched alongside seventy other siblings, most of whom got wiped out by one thing or another. Life in the glen isn't as easy as some make it out to be. We're not all dangling from a fine thread waiting for food to get trapped in our delicately woven webs.

I was born with something of a disadvantage. Right from the outset it was apparent that I had difficulty with my gait. Running too fast made

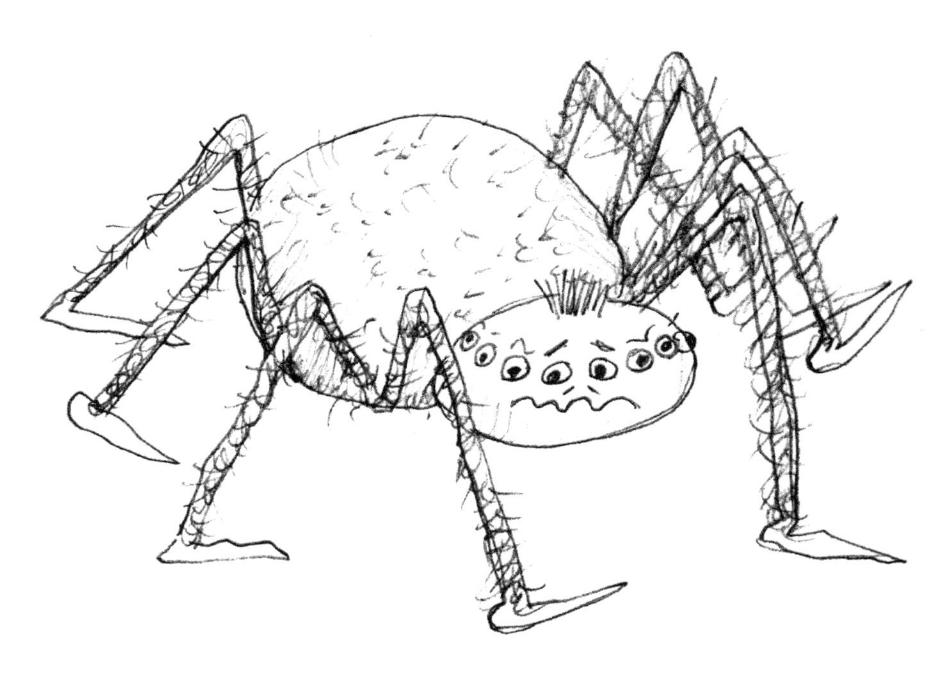

me motion sick. Such is my luck, it turned out that I had eight left feet, hence the name Lefty. My siblings teased me something rotten. I had a miserable time. Added to that, it turned out that I was short-sighted on account of my eyes being too close together. My mother dragged me along to see some medical professional, who got up close and looked into all my eyes. He had incredibly bad breath, so much so I nearly gagged. My mother said it was a good thing I couldn't see him very clearly too because he was incredibly hairy and had a dandruff problem.

So that's me, eight left feet, short-sighted in all of my eyes, all eight of them. Yes, eight legs and eight eyes, oh, and I almost forgot to mention the problem I have with spinning. Well, my legs have something to do with that. If I spin my legs get tangled and then there's the quality of the web. My mum says it's something to do with its stickiness – there's just not enough of it. I'm not painting a great picture of my spider prowess am I? If you were a spider would you have confidence in me?

Such as life was in the glen, I found it increasingly difficult to capture anything let alone eat it. The weight started to fall off and along with that I became weedy and weak. I knew that something was going to have to give, so I decided that there was no option for it but to leave. I cried, out of all eight eyes, when I said goodbye to Mum, but wasn't sad for a moment to be leaving my siblings.

Mum had wrapped a nice fly-piece for me to take on my journey. I didn't really have a clue about where I was going or how I would know when I got there. I set out anyway, heading west in a circular straight line – being left footed tended to make me walk in large circles, so I had a couple of false starts before I got the hang of things. My travels took me far away from the glen, away from the fox and his lair, the badgers and their setts, from the rabbits and their burrows and all the blackbirds, crows and magpies that nested in the trees above where I lived. I wasn't sorry leaving the midges behind either, pesky nippy wee creatures who are only good for mischief. Eventually I came across some rocks. It was a hard climb as they were sharp and covered in slippery moss. I kept going, climbing higher and higher until, exhausted and hungry, I came across the darkened opening of a cave.

It smelled foosty, damp and earthy. It must have been a deep cave because I could hear the steady drip, drip of water from somewhere to the back of it. I stopped and unpacked the fly-piece my mother had lovingly wrapped in her very own web. Looking out from the mouth of the cave, over the tops of the trees of the glen, I sat and munched on delicate crisp fly wings, my favourite. As I ate, fingers of sunlight peeked through the clouds and shone right on the cave entrance. For the first time in my short spider life I felt truly happy. Lefty, I said to myself, this is where you will make your home.

Once I had eaten my fill, I rewrapped the remains of my piece and was just contemplating a wee afternoon siesta, to let my food go down, when I heard a noise. There came a couple of thuds, I saw rocks bouncing down to the bottom of the glen and when I peered over the edge I saw a four-legged body coming towards me. It had red hair on its head and it was breathing heavily and making odd grunting noises. I'd never seen or heard of the like before. For a fleeting moment I thought perhaps this creature might also be left footed like myself, as it was climbing in a very awkward way. I watched as it continued scrambling up the rocks, until finally it reached the mouth of the cave, threw itself on its back and splayed out its limbs, all four of them.

Not quite knowing whether this creature was a threat to me, I decided not to take any chances and so climbed up the entrance of the cave, staying close to the edge. The air seemed sweeter and fresher there – the creature below had an awful pong about it, whiffy to say the least. But as far as I was concerned, it was my cave now. I got here first and was going to make a stake on it. So, I set about trying to spin a web. I tried to take on all the advice that my mother had given me; start from the inside and work out, keep count, spin the thread carefully with my spinnerets (I have two pairs concealed in my tummy), and make it fine not clumpy. Despite all the good advice, it didn't seem to be working. I spun until my stomach ached and my eyes – did I tell you I have eight eyes – bulged. I kept stumbling over my legs, they got all tangled up several times, but that was not going to stop me. I sang a little song to myself to keep my spirits up, 'If at first you don't succeed, try and try and try again.'

I looked back down to the cave floor and could see that the creature was now sitting on two limbs, its two eyes in its head watching me. Was it sizing me up for lunch? Surely not. Maybe it was wondering whether I was left footed like itself, a kindred spirit. I decided not to let my thoughts get in the way of a well-spun web. This was going to be my best creation yet.

I started again, setting my spinnerets in motion and this time it felt easier, something was working for a change. I began to cast my web across the corner of the entrance of the cave, it looked a bit more promising. Hope was rising, a smile spread across my face, and that's not an easy feat, I can tell you. Have you ever seen a spider smile? I launched myself across to where I wanted the width of my web to be and just as I did so … a gust of wind caught me and slammed me into the wall, taking with it a long strand of broken web. It trailed down the wall as the breeze gently buffeted it. My smile disappeared and in its place I set my face to grim determination – which is quite dangerous as I have to take care not to bite myself, these fangs of mine are deadly!

I got back up the rock face again, carefully placing one left foot after the other, then primed my spinnerets and launched. I soared through the air, could hear the rush of air as I flew. This time I made it with a sturdy but fine strand of web to show for my troubles. The spinning got easier. I was making progress. It looked like a real web, one that would capture food, hold my weight and withstand the wind. As I stood marvelling at my creation the creature below had suddenly gone berserk.

Up he jumped whooping and hollering, dancing first on one leg and then another. It was quite a sight to see. My eyes boggled until they couldn't focus. I had to cling on to the web until I found my feet – all eight of them!

He moved up close. I held my breath. He stood right beneath me and looked up directly into my eyes – yes, you know how many! There was a moment where I'm sure we were, well, connected. His breath came in short sharp bursts and made the web quiver. 'Ya beauty,' he said, and then he showed me what I think were his teeth!

I had to stop and look around. 'Are ye talking to me pal?' I shouted, but it was obvious he couldn't hear me. Us spiders use a completely different frequency for communicating.

'Ha! I get it, I get it. Scotland is mine. Oh Rabbie, ye've got them noo, they English huv nae chance.' He then erupted into loud raucous laughter. 'Aye, we'll make them think again.'

And with that, he leapt out of the cave and skipped down the mountainside as nimble as a mountain goat, chanting, 'If at first you don't succeed, try, try and try again,' which I thought rather strange as it was the song I had been singing just ten minutes before he appeared.

Aye, he certainly had a spring in his step that day. I later learned that he had gone and won a battle somewhere nearby, all because he had witnessed me struggling and eventually succeeding to make my first successful web. Apparently I inspired him to give his men the rallying cry: If at first you don't succeed, try, try try again.

Well, who'd have thought it?

Did you know: Spiders create silk from spinneret glands in their abdomen. House spiders can live on average for up to two years.

5

MONKEY BUSINESS

The circus arrived to much fanfare in great wagons pulled by Clydesdale horses. It settled in Ironmills Park, where the big tent was erected before the gleeful eyes of Dalkeith children. Cages of exotic animals sat mostly hidden out of sight. All there was to give them away was the ripe smell of dung and the occasional roar, bellow or chatter from the occupants of the cages.

Motionless, they sat. Hairy bodies all fingers and toes huddling up close against the cold wind that whistled through the cage bars. It had a cruel bite to it, like nothing they had ever experienced before. It was hard to keep warm, their teeth chattered incessantly. Beyond the compound they watched the tall trees bend and weave with the wind.

From across the way the keeper picked his way towards them, treading over the huge wooden tent pegs hammered into the hard ground, sidestepping coils of rope and cages of

sullen-looking animals. Bucket in hand, full of food; his charges could smell it before they saw it. A few broke away from the huddle and prowled the bars, tails erect, gibbering excitedly. As he got closer he shook the bucket, his signal to let them know it was feeding time. Putting the bucket down before the cage door, he searched his pockets for the key to the padlock, talking all the time as he did so. There was an edge to his voice, short tempered and irritated. The animals backed off, watching intently from a distance. Then he opened up.

They pounced on the food; little hairy hands reached in and grabbed, heads twisted this way and that before bodies bounded across the cage to eat in comfort. All the time he kept one eye on the door and another on the lookout for a sudden ambush. This was greeted with outraged screeches and bared teeth, the rest of the troupe joining in, goading with excited babble, leaping up and down, making things worse.

The keeper was distracted as he put out the feed. Simba, the lion in the opposite cage, had a toothache. Rumbling with pain, he charged the bars of the cage, making it rock so violently it threatened to tip over. His rage was escalating, unpredictable at the best of times, and the last thing the circus needed was an angry lion on the loose. A small memory surfaced as the keeper recalled the time Simba had almost mauled his trainer. He decided to get Simba's keeper. Distracted, he left without checking the monkey cage or noticing that it was now without a padlock.

The monkeys weren't daft. This slip was noted. They looked at each other, silently passing it on, smiles behind their eyes. They bunched around the cage door, a pair of little hands slipped around the bolt and carefully edged it back. Before long it was undone and the door lay open, swinging gently in the wind.

The cage soon stood empty, nothing in it but discarded remains of uneaten food. Its occupants covered the ground in a few bounds. They headed straight for the trees and disappeared into the high tree canopy, surprising the black crows of Ironmills Park. They sat, all seven of them, and watched as the circus folk realised their escape. People ran about the grounds, they shouted and called, blew whistles, shook food buckets; for a change, the monkeys were the ones being entertained. From their lofty viewpoint they chattered and fidgeted excitedly.

The hunt was on. Find the monkeys! Three were captured within a short space of time, but the other four scattered, with circus folk and a small band of youngsters from the nearby town of Dalkeith hollering Tarzan's 'call of the wild', hot on their heels.

Although further captures weren't immediate, the majority of them were caught and the circus folk were of the opinion that any remaining escapees would return when they were hungry enough. But not every monkey was THAT hungry.

Odd sightings were soon noted here and there around Dalkeith. All missing items or petty thefts were blamed on 'the monkey'. It had been seen stealing milk bottles from doorsteps, sidling up to vegetable market stalls and making a grab for the goods. It was accused of stealing clothes from washing lines, frightening children and housewives; a face at the window or swinging in the trees at the bottom of the garden. It remained elusive and evaded capture.

It was lunchtime. Jock's stomach was rumbling. He was in a hurry to finish working on the engine, head beneath the bonnet, fiddling with the spark plugs, whistling tunelessly. From the corner of his eye he glimpsed something move at the back of the workshop. A slight but quick movement, one that leaves you thinking, 'Did I imagine that?' He looked up but saw nothing but dust motes dancing in the window light.

Something definitely moved across the other side of the room. He heard a sound, a chink of an oil can moving, the unmistakable sound of a jar resettling into place. Keeping his head still, his eyes flicked to the direction of the sound and caught sight of the rear end of a small, nimble

monkey disappearing into the office, its long tail high in the air like a periscope. Wiping his hands on his overalls, Jock moved to the office door. Holding his breath, he peered in.

It was sitting on the desk with its back to him. Light from the window made its silver down glow, giving it a glamorous allure. It was engrossed, small hands working hard to break into Jock's lunch box. The lid flew off with a bang. The animal screeched and leapt backwards, knocking over jars and tins lined up on a shelf, which tumbled and shattered. The creature shrieked again and jumped across the room to land on top of a metal locker with a clang. Jock barrelled in, bellowing and shouting, more at the mess than the monkey. It wasn't the best of moves. From its vantage point the monkey, eyes wide, squealed, picked up the nearest objects and lobbed them at Jock.

Cam belts, oily rags, a box of spark plugs and a couple of car manuals came across the room at speed, the monkey shouting toothy insults as it did so. When the ammunition ran out it briefly turned its face to the wall and aimed its bottom in Jock's direction, looking back at him, pointing at it and making as if to laugh.

'You cheeky monkey!' Jock gasped, yet at the same time admiring its boldness, despite the mess and the awful smell the creature had about it. He slammed the door shut and went across the road to the grocers. He had a plan.

The monkey hunched over the plate, its nimble fingers stuffing apple and banana into its mouth faster than he could chew. It ate as if it hadn't seen food for a week, which was probably the case. An intrigued Jock looked on, careful not to be seen. He continued to put food out for Pongo, the name he had given the monkey on account of its smell. By the end of the week Pongo sat close enough for Jock to hand him fruit and when he was done he settled into the old car seat among the nest of rags Jock had brought in for him. It became something of a comfortable alliance.

The circus that Pongo belonged to had long since moved on. The local newspaper reported that the circus 'had been reunited with all its missing monkeys'. Jock was secretly pleased. He had become quite attached to his new friend, who now liked to sit on his shoulder and play.

When the colder months drew in, Jock worried. He wanted to make sure that Pongo was warm enough, and the garage was a draughty place. He asked his wife, Joan, if he could bring Pongo home but was met with an outright refusal. 'I'll not have a dirty, smelly monkey in my house.' Jock knew better than to push his luck, his wife could sulk for days. So he resigned himself to keeping Pongo at the garage. As a result, Jock spent more time at work. Finally, his wife relented and agreed to allow Pongo home.

Things went well at first. Pongo tucked into his meals on the kitchen units while the family ate their supper at the table. Joan knitted him a jumper in Jock's favourite football team colours to keep him warm. Pongo delighted in hiding his treats in its deep pockets. Joan, in spite of herself, warmed to Pongo. She carried him like he was a small baby and sang him lullabies just like she did her own children when they were small. Best of all, when Jock settled in his chair by the fire to read the paper, Pongo took to grooming what was left of Jock's hair. Family life was comfortable and rewarding, Pongo thrived on being the centre of attention.

The change came when Barry arrived on the scene. Barry was their 8-year-old grandson. His parents had moved back into the area to be near family and to have help with childcare, another child was on the way. Increasingly, Barry spent more time with his grandparents. Pongo played quite happily with Barry at first, and it seemed like a wonderful friendship was in the making. But Barry had a mean streak, he would pull Pongo's tail, poke him, pinch him and make sudden movements that made Pongo skittish and fearful. It didn't take long before Pongo took great exception to Barry. He chewed up his toys and threw them out the window, screeched loudly when the boy entered the room, and careered around the furniture and curtains. Barry often chased Pongo, and this drove him wild. On several occasions Jock had to shout at Barry to 'leave the poor creature alone'. Once he caught Barry yanking hard on Pongo's tail and gave him such a row that he locked himself in the bathroom for several hours. The day came when Barry cornered Pongo. Gleefully, he poked him with Grandma's umbrella and laughed when Pongo shrieked.

In a fraught effort to escape, Pongo launched himself at Barry, who caught him in his arms. Struggling against the child's ever tightening grip, Pongo bit Barry on the arm. The boy screamed louder and longer than need be. Pongo leapt up to the top of the curtain rail and also began to screech wildly, bringing Jock and his wife running.

A decision had to be made. 'Surely you can't choose a monkey over your grandson?' Jock's son argued. Jock and Joan talked long into the night.

When the lights went out Joan cried softly as her husband tossed and turned in his sleep. In the room next door, Pongo curled up in the little bed that Jock had made for him, blissfully unaware of how his fate was to unfold.

A couple of days later Pongo was removed and rehomed. One of Jock's employees, Simon, agreed to take him. Jock and Joan seemed, on the face of it, to take it all quietly and with good nature. The house was silent as Joan packed up his belongings into a little suitcase, all those hand-knitted jumpers and dolls that Pongo loved. The sight of Pongo's anxious face looking out at them from the back of the car haunted Joan for many a day long after Pongo had moved on. She felt as though she had lost a family member, her household companion, her confidant. Jock, on the other hand, refused to speak about it, loading all his sadness and loss into building model aeroplanes in the garden shed.

But this wasn't the end of Pongo's friendship with Jock and Joan. His new owner, Simon, often brought Pongo to work to help out in the garage. In turn, Joan's visits to the garage increased, 'to keep Pongo company' she would say.

As for Simon, he was devoted to Pongo and took him everywhere with him. The monkey never wanted for anything. Nothing was too much bother and Pongo in turn adored Simon. He lived to a ripe old age in Restalrig with Simon and became a legend in his own lifetime.

This is a true story and is remembered by some elderly residents of Dalkeith. Photographs of Pongo are still held by The Advertiser.

6

THE DRAKE'S TALE

Mrs McGregor didn't set out to have any of her animals. She claimed they just found their way to her by some circumstance or other.

Take the chickens, for example. After a visit to a children's nursery one day, she found herself heading home with four chickens. It happened so suddenly that even Mrs McGregor was surprised. She recalled the lady at the nursery saying that she was desperate to find them homes and the next thing she knew there they were in a box on her car passenger seat watching her as she drove home. Fortunately, Mr McGregor was away on business at the time so she was able to hide them in the garage until suitable housing, a coop, could be found.

How the duck came to the house was an entirely different story. Once a year Mrs McGregor employed the services of a gardener to prune the hedges and trees. Mr McAllister had done the job for years. Every autumn without fail, he rolled up in his truck laden with gardening equipment and got to work, whistling loudly as he did so.

Now, it just so happened that Mr McAllister kept domestic birds, too. He had an assortment of chickens: white stars, bluebells, buff Orpingtons and Silkies. He liked the Silkies best on account of their fluffy feathers and weird hairdos.

'They look like they're wearing dandelion clocks that have been shaved into Mohican hairdos,' he once mused. He also kept ducks, mostly Indian Runners, 'but they're no half as much fun as the chooks,' he claimed. So it was inevitable that their conversation would stray on to their domestic birds.

'I see you've a coop that yer no using,' said Mr McAllister, indicating with his chin.

'Ach, yes. I bought that when I left the council, but the girls (the chickens) dinnae like it.'

'Well, if yer interested, I've a duck that would make guid use o' it.'

'Aye?' said Mrs McGregor, half listening. 'How's that?'

'It's no happy where it is. Such a guid-natured critter too but ma flock just huvnae ta'en tae him. He's quite a duck ye ken. The ithers have been bullying it something rotten. He has nae friends. Whenever he goes near any o' them, they set aboot him. Noo a' the feathers oan the back o' his neck are missing.'

'But how's that?'

'It's where they've pecked him.'

Mrs McGregor gasped.

'It looks richt sair. A've never seen such a sad and lonely critter.' Mr McAllister paused to look at Mrs McGregor. Her eyes had moistened, she clutched her chest and was now giving him her full and undivided attention.

Clearing his throat and looking straight into her eyes Mr McAllister made his heartfelt plea, 'You wouldnae perhaps consider …'

'I'd love to but …'

'I ken you'd take the greatest o' care with him,' he paused to blow his nose, 'being a duck of such a vulnerable and tender nature.' A long silent moment passed between them.

'Of course,' said Mrs McGregor, 'it wid depend on how ma girls react to him … and my husband wid huv to agree.' Mr McAllister removed his cap reverently, his eyes almost pleading. 'I'll have a wee blether wi' him and let you ken.' She turned to head back into the house.

'I could bring him round this evening if you like,' Mr McAllister called as she disappeared through the back door.

Later that afternoon, Mr McAllister received a phone call from Mrs McGregor saying that she was happy to take the duck. What she didn't mention was that her husband wasn't entirely convinced that it was a good idea but, as usual, had been overruled, or perhaps overrun, by Mrs McGregor's enthusiasm. The duck was to be dropped off at the house that evening.

At 6 p.m. prompt, Mr McAllister's white truck drew up outside the house. Mrs McGregor observed from her kitchen window with a sense of growing excitement. Over the course of the afternoon she had imagined what it would be like having a little duck in her flock. She had built up quite a rosy picture: she could see it waddling round the garden, its little yellow bill nibbling at the slugs and snails. She watched as Mr McAllister carefully carried something from the cab of the truck and walk along the full length of the vehicle. Eagerly she went to meet him at the back gate but was rather taken aback when she saw him come through it.

The duck under his arm was enormous, not at all what she had expected by a long stretch of the imagination. In her mind's eye her version of the duck was the type you saw on the pond in the local park. One of mallard proportions. The duck before her was more akin to the size of a Jack Russell terrier, if not bigger.

It had a large, red, warty-looking mask around its eyes and above its beak. On top of its head it wore a strange crest of feathers. The rest of its body was a mass of glossy white with varying degrees of blue-black feathers.

Mrs McGregor viewed it with a sense of trepidation. When she noticed its webbed feet and its strong sharp claws she became considerably alarmed. She didn't recall the ducks at the local pond looking this scary. Mr McAllister followed her gaze. 'For grabbing tree branches and roosting,' he said, as if trying to reassure himself. He could tell that Mrs McGregor might take some convincing.

'Are you sure that's a … duck?' asked Mrs McGregor with her eye firmly fixed on its claws.

'Positive. It's a Muscovy duck. A richt timid Muscovy duck an all.' Mrs McGregor shifted uncomfortably from one foot to the other, eyeing it warily.

'What's its name?'

'We cry him Ducky.' There followed a rather long and uneasy pause.

'Ducky it is then.' No sooner had she spoken than Mr McAllister swiftly deposited Ducky into the coop. He gave her instructions on its feed and left before she changed her mind.

Early the next morning, Mrs McGregor was out feeding the girls and had made a special meal of lettuce, tomatoes and fish bits for Ducky. She placed it inside his coop along with fresh water. Ducky made no attempt to move, just sat forlornly on his perch. He continued in this way for two weeks.

A concerned Mrs McGregor kept a close eye on him and worked hard to put interesting treats in his foodstuff to tempt him off his perch. 'Poor thing,' she would croon, 'you've really nothing to worry about here. The girls won't hurt you.'

On the third week a change occurred, Ducky ventured out of his coop and into the run. It was a small success but, despite the fact that the coop was left open to the garden, Ducky stayed resolutely within the confines of the run. It seemed that he preferred the safety of his small caged world. Mrs McGregor was patient and kind with him. She thought it quite sad that Ducky was afraid of the world beyond and made it her mission to bring about a positive change.

At first the girls stalked around the pen, eyeing him suspiciously. When Ducky made no attempt to leave, the girls soon forgot about him and carried on scratching up the garden and clucking among themselves.

Then, one day, Ducky made a bid for freedom. He ventured past the open coop door, waddling slowly out into the centre of the garden. At first, the girls stood stock still in disbelief then, once recovered, they lifted their beaks to the sky, screeching and squawking their displeasure.

'Top chook' Gertie took things further. Outraged, she ran at Ducky, wings scooped forward like a big, wide, hooped dress, making her look bigger than she was. Ducky stood his ground and hissed, then turned his huge back on her and waddled away. Flummoxed, Gertie tried again, and again, but was faced with the same response. After several days the girls tired of trying to intimidate Ducky and ignored him. Ducky took to perching on top of the garden bench, quietly watching garden life going on around him.

But Ducky did find a way to prove himself worthy of the flock's love and adoration. One day, several gulls had landed in the garden, scavenging for food. They were busily tucking into the chicken feed, while in the background the girls made their annoyance known in the only way they knew, when suddenly Ducky slid off his perch.

For a duck of his size he could move swiftly when he put his mind to it. In a flash he was off the bench, hissing and flapping his wings. There was no mistaking that he meant business. The startled gulls didn't know what to make of it. Hastily, they took off with Ducky in hot pursuit honking loudly. After that the girls took him under their wings and Ducky became one of the flock.

Ducky continued to keep watch from his perch on top of the bench. He would stay there all day and sometimes well into the late evening, his outline standing out against the twilight. Often Mrs McGregor would have to coax him down and into the safety of the coop. Years passed and it just so happened that Mrs McGregor noticed that Ducky was getting larger. It got to the stage where he had to squeeze through the coop door to get in.

When excited he wagged his tail from side to side and see-sawed his neck back and forth, the feathers on the top of his head cresting as he went. Mostly he got excited when it was feeding time and he would take the lion's share. But as time went by, Ducky wanted or perhaps needed more than the small flock of friends could offer. He had company but he wanted a mate, a Mrs Muscovy. He became very sad. No matter how much the girls tried, Ducky could not be cheered up.

It came to Mrs McGregor's attention. She would watch him from her kitchen window, his sadness evident. Reluctantly she decided it was time Ducky was found a new home, one that would suit all his needs. With a heavy heart, she started to make enquiries, contacting farmers, duck enthusiasts and bird sanctuaries, but nobody seemed to want him. 'He's too big,' some said. 'That's not a duck,' asserted others. Time passed and Ducky got bigger and sadder.

Once a month, Mrs McGregor went to the farmers' grain store to buy layers pellets – chicken food. In the backyard of the store there was a large fenced area where chickens and ducks were kept for anyone to purchase. On this one particular occasion Mrs McGregor had an idea. Perhaps the store would be interested in taking Ducky – surely one of their customers would have the right room and conditions for him? With this in mind she made enquiries. She approached the counter and stood quietly before the man working the till.

He was preoccupied with stacking the shelves behind him and failed to notice her. After a while she cleared her throat loudly. 'Errhem. Hello. I have a duck.'

The man behind the counter carried on filling the shelves, half listening. Or so it seemed.

'He's a large duck,' she continued. 'And now I fear that he is in need of a home more suited to duck life.'

'Oh,' said the young man, rather distracted.

'You wouldnae be interested in taking him wid you? To see if any of your customers might be able to accommodate him? I see you already huv ducks and chickens in your pen over there.' Mrs McGregor stood, shoulders squared and looked the shop attendant right in the eye. A moment passed between them. He could tell that she was not going to just go away.

'I'll go and ask the boss,' he muttered with a sigh. 'He's oot the back.' And before Mrs McGregor could say anything more, he retreated.

Less than five minutes later, he reappeared. 'Aye, but it wid be best if you cud bring the duck this afternoon. Do you think you cud de that?'

Staggered, Mrs McGregor nodded. 'Aye. Aye of course, I'll huv him here by 5.30 p.m. at the latest. See yoos later then.' Quickly she left the shop and returned home, thinking to herself, how on earth am I going to get Ducky here?

Ducky was of such a size that to merely put him in the car without anything to contain him would probably mean causing an accident. She knew he wouldn't oblige and sit still in a safety belt. A box was required, but what would be suitable? All the cardboard boxes she had were far too small.

The solution came to her when she got home. Suddenly she remembered the large cardboard box that the new hoover came in. When her 8-year-old son saw it he pleaded with her to let him have it. Boxes of that size were hard to come by. Cameron had plans. He fashioned it into a rocket ship complete with toilet roll engines covered in silver foil, a control panel and windows with yellow cellophane. It certainly looked the part, so much so that Cameron had actually spent a couple of nights sleeping in it, dreaming that he was floating from space, captain of his very own rocket ship.

When he came home from school that day Mrs McGregor sat him down and told him that the grain store would take Ducky that afternoon. 'They'll find Ducky the home that he needs but the only snag is how to get him there.' Without hesitation, Cameron piped up, 'Can we no send Ducky off in my rocket ship?'

Clapping her hands in glee, Mrs McGregor congratulated her son on his clever idea. Soon they were busy manoeuvring Ducky into his very own rocket ship. It wasn't as easy as it seemed. Ducky was elusive and fast, despite his heavy features. After ten minutes of chasing him around the back garden, Cameron and Mrs McGregor decided to change tack and use cunning. A tasty treat was planted, or an 'incentive' as Mrs McGregor coined it. They stood back and waited, watching from the kitchen window. Ducky never could resist dried meal worms and walked straight into the rocket ship. Once in, the end was closed up and the box carefully lifted into the back of the car. Mrs McGregor started the engine and drove slowly but carefully to the grain store.

Ducky was most displeased with his incarceration and took to bashing the inside of the box with his beak. He honked and hissed and tried to flap his wings. He made such a rumpus that she was sure that he was going to break out and flap about the car. Twenty minutes later Mrs McGregor carefully parked up. She asked the man on the till if she could back her car into the chicken run.

'But why? It's only a duck. Surely you cuid just lift him in?'

'Err, no. I think he's a wee bit distressed. It wid be much better this way.'

'Och, very well then.' Begrudgingly, he lifted down the keys and made his way out to the gate. Slowly and carefully, Mrs McGregor backed the car into the chicken run. Then she opened the boot and tipped the rocket ship at an angle in such a way that Ducky slid out of it and landed on his bottom. Then he was up on his webbed feet in a flash. He stood in the centre of the pound stretching his neck and lifting his head skywards, wings outstretched and flapping furiously as he stamped and honked.

The flock had never seen the like. One hundred and fifty chickens stood stock still, looking on, beaks open, shocked.

'Is that a duck?' It was more of a statement than a question; the look on the assistant's face spoke volumes.

'Aye,' Mrs McGregor's tone was quite unapologetic. 'That he certainly is.' Then she smartly

shut the car boot, waved goodbye to Ducky and drove off, leaving the rocket ship in the middle of the chicken yard looking very much as if it had just landed.

It was less than a couple of days later that Ducky was found a new home on the Laird of Middleton's estate. It has a huge lake with an island at its centre whereupon many a duck has made its home, including Ducky, who is now king of all he surveys and a very, very happy one at that.

Did you know: Muscovy ducks can live for up to thirty years.

7

DUNDEE'S DRAGON

If you ever happen to pass through Dundee city centre it is quite likely that you will come across the statue of its very own dragon, complete with a flame and inimitable smile. But don't be fooled into thinking that this is just a mythical creature made up to intrigue the tourists. The dragon is very much part and parcel of Dundee's heritage and here is an insight into the story as passed down by my grandfather, Fergus, who told it something like this:

> Things would have been verra different had I had masel' a son or twa. As it turned oot, I ended up wi' nine lassies. All o' us living virtually one on top of anither in the auld farm hoose. Their Mother, Celia, indulged them of course. Brocht them up tae think they would marry a handsome prince, or rich laird at the very least, and be whisked awa' tae bide in a castle. There they imagined

they would live oot the rest of their days in luxury wi' handmaidens a-plenty.

And so, because of this, the hoose is an awfie mess, a richt guddle. None o' the lassies hae a clue aboot hoosekeeping or hoosework, all they can think aboot is fine dresses, hairstyles, cosmetics and the next up and coming ball. Oh and then there's the shoes – I despair! I'm sure they could fill a whole dungeon wi' their shoes.

> But aside from the poor hoosekeeping, cooking and constant bickering ower whose tapestry is the best, they're no' a bad lot and things hae improved since I had a privy installed just for me. The one good thing aboot ma dochters is that they are all verra biddable and aye at my beck and call.

Yet despite the fact that Fergus, son of Fergus of Pittempton, Dundee, owned the land as far as the eye could see, he was not fully aware of what was on his land or how it was used. You see, he was a rather lazy landowner and left it very much up to his tenants to work while he sat back and ate the profits or spent his money on dresses and shoes for his daughters.

He was aware of where the majority of fertile lands lay and knew that over to the west the land was less than good. In fact, it was rather boggy and useless to a farmer. A marsh! Indeed, the only thing it did have going for it was its well. Water drawn from it was the sweetest, purest water ever tasted. Some claimed it had restorative powers and was capable of giving you some oomph when you felt less than oomphy. According to Fergus, 'It's because o' the well we got intae this mess.'

It all started because Fergus had a headache. He got it on account of something he ate that didn't agree with him. He felt so awful that he had to lie down, at which point everyone started fussing. All he really wanted was to lie down in a darkened room until he felt better, but no, in and out they all came, plying him with unctions and potions and then squabbling among themselves as to who had the best suggestion. So, in the end he asked for some water from the well in the marsh, just to keep them occupied and get them out of his way.

Marion, the oldest of the nine daughters, went first. She should have only taken forty minutes at most. An hour passed, then another half hour and still no sight of her. So Mary, the next oldest, went out to the marsh, and when she didn't return, Madelaine went in her stead. Fergus remained lying in a darkened room, blissfully unaware that his daughters, one by one, had gone off to the marsh to fetch water for him and not returned.

What he was to find out later was that a creature, a monster of a dragon, had taken up residence in the marsh. It had already chomped its way through a flock of wading birds before his first daughter turned up, and after it had snacked on her, the luncheon kept on coming. All of his bonnie, naive, sweet lassies made their way to their doom that day, and for what? To get their old ailing father and a draught of the well water that he really didn't need.

Meredith, the youngest, was the last to have her fate sealed. Who knows what she saw when she got to the well. Perhaps she happened to spy something floating in the water or something among the bullrushes. Imagine if you will, there she is, stepping closer to the water's edge to get a better look and ... the shock and horror when she sees what she sees. A shoe, a blue shoe. Not just any shoe, but one of the new pairs that she and her sister Myra, had squabbled over that very morning. There it is, floating in the water, a blue stain spreading out like ink across the surface. The shoe that belonged to her dearest, bonnie sister, Myra with the long hair and crooked teeth.

Then, Meredith lets out a blood-curdling scream and starts greetin. Lifting up her petticoats and skirts, she attempts to run in her new purple shoes away from the marsh but the heels get stuck in the mud, she trips … And alas, her cries alert the dragon, who was still snacking on Myra.

The dragon was quick and fairly light on its feet. Despite the mists surrounding the marsh, it was able to fix its beady eyes upon its 'prize', although Fergus was more inclined to think that it was able to smell where she was as 'she did tend tae be rather heavy handed wi' the lavender water'. He claimed even he could smell her before she arrived. Poor Meredith only managed to cover some 300 yards before the dragon had started to wrap his jaws around her – and still she squealed and shrieked.

Her desperate cries alerted the local tenant farmers living not far from the marsh. They huddled together, afraid of what was causing all the stramash. Only one from that group was gallus enough to take up his sword, jump on his horse and head, full gallop, towards the din, closely followed by a timorous crowd eager for a bit of excitement as a break from their monotonous existence.

It was Martin of Pittempton, a farm labourer, who had taken up the challenge. He may have been poor but he was strong of heart and brawny, too. Onwards he charged to take up the fight with the dragon, followed at a safe distance by the other tenants. By the time he got up close, he was just in time to witness Meredith's feet, complete with purple shoes, disappearing down the back of the dragon's throat.

A red rage took hold of Martin for, unbeknownst to Fergus, he and Meredith had been meeting in secret and had planned to run away and wed. (She had ordered a new dress and shoes (pink) especially for the occasion.) Martin loved her more than life itself. He raised his sword and swore to avenge his beloved Meredith, then charged at the dragon, piercing and jabbing at its thick scaly body. He twisted and turned his horse this way and that, narrowly missing the dragon's snapping jaws, and an incredible fight ensued. Hour upon hour they fought until they reached Dighty Burn. The tenant farmers had started to take bets on who was going to win. Sandwiches and drinks were being handed around. After a short breather and lunch break, Martin set to again.

Fear was not something that entered into Martin's mind. He was brave and gallus. He wanted revenge, he wanted the dragon's head and was not going to stop until he had succeeded.

The two were evenly matched. Martin was young, swift and filled with a rage that fuelled his ambition to destroy the beast. The dragon, although strong and powerful, had a bellyful of birds and all nine of Fergus' daughters. They slowed him down, and he wanted nothing more than to sleep and take time to let the contents of his stomach sort themselves out. The two of them continued to wrangle and fight for many hours but Martin was not one to give up. At a place called Brigfoot the dragon began to show signs of tiring, his reflexes were getting slower. Sensing this, Martin pushed harder, his blows now beginning to connect and inflict damage. The fight sprawled on to the plain before the rise of Balludaron hill. At this point the crowd swelled, they could see the dragon was faltering or 'draigled at Baldragon', as it was later claimed. They became positively excited as the fight continued on to Strathmartine, cheering and whistling as they went.

Finally, Martin reined in his horse to stand squarely in front of the dragon. Looking it right in its eerie cuttlefish-like yellow eyes, he held his sword aloft defiantly.

'I will avenge ma beloved Meredith. You, despicable dragon, have eaten yer last maiden and drawn yer last breath.'

And with that he lunged straight at the surprised and rather bemused beast, for no one had ever taken him on before and succeeded, especially not a mere human. While the dragon was busy musing on this fact, Martin's horse stumbled and threw him high into the air. Distracted, the dragon seized the opportunity to grab himself another wee snack and swiftly gulped down the horse, saddle and all. He had momentarily forgotten all about Martin, who was now descending at a rapid rate with the crowd behind him chanting 'Strike Martin! Strike Martin!'

Martin landed directly on the dragon's head and with the force of the fall and his own might, plunged the sword through the top of the dragon's skull and killed him outright. It toppled over onto a huge flat stone and Martin tumbled off. When he got to his feet he stood before the dragon and looked on as a great pool of green blood began to seep from its wound. Its eyes, still open, blinked one last time and from its mouth a small flame and a puff of smoke erupted. The crowd was ecstatic and, cheering and shouting wildly, they danced on the boggy marsh.

Martin, exhausted, fell to his knees and sobbed. Grief came over him like a great blanket. His tears streamed down his face and fell to the floor where he knelt. He cried and cried until soon a small pool of water began to form. Still the tears continued to fall. He shed so many that a spring appeared. Years after the slaying of the dragon the locals named the spring 'the nine maidens well', and as if to prove that the water had come from salty tears, to this day the water is still a lot saltier that any fresh water spring should be. Martin went on to receive a posthumous sainthood for his act of bravery. This came about because a certain Bishop David de Berham dedicated a church to Martin, which in turn caused him to be sainted in 1249. But it was no consolation for losing the love of his life. Apparently he never fell in love again.

Others, on hearing of the tragedy, have put their own stamp on that place by placing sculptured stones there. One is referred to as St Martin's Stone and is found at Balecco, and another is to be found at Strathmartine. If you look very, very carefully near St Martin's Stone, there is a stone with a symbol of a pictish beastie on it that marks the actual spot where the dragon was slain, hence the expression 'kill'd at Martin's Stane'.

As for Fergus the farmer, he and his wife Celia sold up and moved away. They couldn't bear to live in the farmhouse without their beautiful daughters. Gravestones dedicated to their daughters' memories could be found in a wee kirkyard between the Dighty and Craigmill Road and lasted well into the nineteenth century. Fergus became the subject of nasty rumours that claimed he tried to shed tears that he didn't have and as a result ended up shrivelling up and dying. Nonsense. He lived to a ripe old age and moved to the heart of the city of Dundee.

Dundee city erected a statue of the dragon and sited it at the east end of the High Street many centuries after the event. The statue, conceived by Alistair Smart and crafted by Tony Morrow, is affectionately known as the Dundee Dragon and is still enjoyed to this day.

8

MORAGUS THE HAGGIS

Moragus was a haggis
one of the lowland kind
Descended from an ancient clan
Some of whom were blind

Up and down the rushy glens
and round the lochs she ran
Searching in the gorse and heather
for her son, called Dan

Now Dan was quite a funny sort
He didn't like cold weather
He hated mist and rain and snow
and always carried an umbrella

Sometimes he wore a macintosh
and a funny looking bunnet
Come rain he wears his wellingtons
and a sporran round his stomach

They like to feed on earwigs
and slimy slugs and toads
and if you're not too careful
they'll nibble on your toes

Most folk think they live in holes
underneath the ground
Or in the darkest deepest caves
where bones lie all around

But those of us 'in the know'
We can plainly see
You've all been looking in the wrong place
For Haggis live in trees

(Except for Moragus, she bides in a litter bin
in Holyrood Palace!)

9

MAGICAL JOURNEY TO THE ISLE OF SKYE

The last person to see Granny was my sister. She claimed she watched her turn into a butterfly – a tortoiseshell with a flash of warm orange. It fluttered away over the garden wall, heading off in the direction of the Forth Road Bridge. Granny had always said when her time came she would take herself off, and fly away like a butterfly: she loved butterflies. None of us ever saw her again. My only consolation was being given an amber nugget from her favourite necklace. It looked like a barley sugar lozenge, golden amber, with a hint of orange, the same as the butterfly, and it was all I had left to remind me of her.

Granny was an unusual, wonderful woman – resourceful, ebullient, generous with love and laughter. She would delight us with her stories, some funny, some weird, but all filled with warmth and kindness. Once you'd met her, you'd never forget her. She relished the unusual, embraced the quirky, and savoured all things mischievous. She was not a conventional woman, not by a long stretch of the imagination.

Her expansive carpet bag was an endless source of intrigue – once, she pulled out from its depths a cockerel's spur, a pair of men's oversized Y-fronts and a spurtle. Our mother was aghast, but Granny just laughed, exposing her loose-fitting dentures.

Everyone knew Granny for miles around. She was often the first face to have seen them when they were new. With a smile as wide as the Firth of Forth, she cleaned, swaddled and blessed the babe, before handing it to the mother. As a midwife, she had welcomed hundreds of babies into this world. 'Each child,' she would say, 'has added to my mountain of joy.'

As the years passed, my memories of her – and her amber nugget – stayed with me. Occasionally, I would spot a butterfly – a tortoiseshell with its distinctive pattern of orange, red and yellow – caught in the sunlight. It would appear at times when I was sad or anxious, or during moments of pure joy, like my niece's christening. On seeing it, I would think of Granny and her words, 'all will be well', would come to mind.

I followed the same trade as many of the women in our family – midwifery of one sort or another. My path was the less conventional one, I preferred a more nurturing approach and so became a doula.* I must have helped bring 120 babies into the world by now.

Age and hard work have taken their toll, and I consider it a necessity to take myself away every now and then: to rest, recharge and reflect. After all, I'm no good to anyone if I don't. I always hold in my mind's eye that mountain of joy to which Granny often referred.

This time, it was an impulsive choice – or so it seemed. I wanted sea air, mountains and something different to the norm. I'd scoured the Internet and nothing really appealed, but then I came across a postcard left at a random table at my local cafe. It read: 'Magical journeys to the Isle of Skye'. It seemed to offer everything I was looking for. So I booked, there and then, before I had a change of heart.

A fortnight later, I found myself on a bus, heading north. Jostled among a myriad of tourists, managing my cumbersome bags, queueing, waiting with my ticket at the ready, and then finally being herded off at the other end into luminous sunshine and cloudless blue skies.

I took a taxi to the wee cottage I had rented for the week. When I stepped out of the car, something fluttered to my left, just outside my peripheral vision. The taxi driver set my suitcase down on the pavement, and the fluttering stopped as whatever it was landed, opening its black velvety wings to show the delicate tracing of a beautiful tortoiseshell butterfly.

I spent the first couple of days wandering round the Cuillin Hills, or venturing into local towns. At Staffin, I marvelled at the views as the Old Man of Storr dominated the skyline, silhouetted before the sloping buttresses of Trotternish, with its huge landslides and dramatic jagged cliffs. I was particularly drawn to Elgol, perched on a steep hillside with its hairpin bend leading down to the pier. There I sampled the local fare: fresh fish and hot buttered scones.

I loved the soothing sound of the sea, the island's breathtaking views, the colour and texture of the landscape, velvet greens mingled with purple heather and yellow gorse. For the first two nights, I had the best sleep I had had in years. But on the third night, a strange wind blew in from the sea. I felt restless and fractious but couldn't work out why. Sleep evaded me. I lay awake absorbing night sounds: the haunting song of curlew, the squabbles of greylag geese and the bellowing bark of grey seal. During the early hours, I dozed, half awake, drifting in and out, but the spell was broken by a knock at my door.

I lay there trying to figure out whether I had really heard it or whether it was something I had dreamt. It came again. Tap tap tap. This time, I sensed the urgency in the knocking.

It was 3 a.m. Outside it was dark. Who would call on me at this time? The knock came again. I stretched, got up, put on my dressing gown and opened the door. There, before me, stood a tall man.

'Oh, my!' I said, taking him in from the floor and up, up, up to his face. He was dressed from head to foot in a green outfit. He looked like he had emerged out of the stone wall that surrounded the cottage and was covered in a luscious soft moss. On his head he wore a cap with a jaunty feather. Around him gleamed tiny shafts of light, shimmering with each movement. He bent down to look me in the eye, and without uttering a word, grabbed hold of my hand and pulled me out into the cold night.

I couldn't tell you why I didn't resist or shout out, it was as if he had taken my voice when he had taken my hand. Only the wildcats, hiding among the rocks and trees, saw us pass. He clasped my hand tight as we made our way across the moor, him striding ahead. It was difficult to keep up. My chest constricted, my breath was starting to come in short, tight bursts. I couldn't think straight. I thought of my impending retirement, how this night-time walk didn't fit in with my plans, that my old bones just weren't what they used to be, and why was I trying to run?

At times I stumbled, but that seemed the least of my problems. I couldn't catch up enough to look him in the face and ask, 'Who are you? Where are you taking me and why?' We had now gone past the wee shop, past the pier and the little boats that bobbed up and down with the lapping waves. We travelled on and on, until I no longer recognised where we were. All the familiar landmarks were gone and in their stead were a confusion of steep pathways through which the wind stirred, with a softened purr to its whisper.

Shadows danced wild and unbound without matching movements around them. There was only one long shadow moving along at a swift pace … mine. And still we moved on, fleet down steep inclines. When we came to a fork in the road, pointing to the right was a sign of a butterfly. A tortoiseshell butterfly. Granny? I thought, and heard her voice, 'All will be well.'

I felt myself relax a little. Then, a fragment of a story Granny had told us came to mind, one about a strange journey not unlike this one. I realised this must be one of the fairy folk – he was much, much taller than I'd imagined. I had always thought they were wee, no taller than my knee.

I knew they were powerful beings, not to be messed with or challenged, so I surrendered to this strange experience as best I could. At some point I tripped and fell, my blackened feet bleeding in places. He stopped, loosened his grip and helped me up. When I looked him in the eye I saw concern, kindness. Although no words had passed between us, I sensed I was safe. After that, our pace slowed.

After what felt like another hour of walking, we climbed a slope into an altogether different place, unlike anything I had seen on the island.

We entered a cave. At first it seemed dark and dank, but the deeper we went into its heart, the wider it became. The walls had changed colour from brown to honey to a rose pink. We climbed a section of narrow stone stairs until we reached a huge wooden door that bore signs of age, but didn't look as if it was often used. It yawned open to reveal an elaborate pool filled with golden fish and sprinkles of rose petals. All around the courtyard orange and myrtle trees blossomed, their distinct aromas mingling, and butterflies flitted amidst the flowers and trees. I felt heady and happy, all my tumbling thoughts stopped. A breeze wafted through the door, lifting blossom high into the air. I watched the petals rise and fall like confetti. Then I noticed I was in the courtyard of a huge rose-coloured palace, its walls cutting imposing outlines against the dimly lit sky. How can this be, I thought, a castle within a cave?

The fairy-man led me through an opening into the palace, and along a tiled corridor adorned with tapestries and paintings. Then we entered a sumptuous room. It had low ceilings, and all around the room candles flickered in sconces. In the centre was a large bed, upon which lay a beautiful young woman. Her earrings struck me immediately as they were exactly the same shape and size of Granny's amber nugget. One look at her, and I knew why I was there. Her belly was as round as a drum. She looked tired and flushed, her hair plastered to her head. Their baby had been trying to be born for some time now. The fairy-man went to her side and took her hand. He looked entreatingly from me to her.

I got to work, listened to her belly, then rubbed her back. By fortune I found, in my dressing gown pocket, some barley sugar sweeties, perhaps from a time when I had delivered another child into the world. I handed one to the young woman, mimed a chewing action and encouraged her to do the same. Then I waited. Suddenly she sat up, placed her hands on her belly and strained forward. She began to tremble. Magical streams of light filled the room and soon after, a child was born. A boy fairy. I checked his tiny form, wrapped him in soft linen, said a blessing for his long life and handed him over to his proud mother. Both parents beamed with joy, their child arrived at last.

It was then I noticed a movement at the far end of the room. It was a slight, delicate motion, the fluttering orangey wings of a small tortoiseshell butterfly. It danced towards us and landed on the bedstead at the end of the bed.

But the moment of joy was interrupted as the mother quickly handed the child over to the fairy-man, her brow furrowing and her belly beginning to tremble. I bent once more to listen closely: then, smiling, I held up two fingers. Two fairy babies! More magical light filled the room, the butterfly danced, I rubbed her back, urging her to chew the barley sugar – and soon another baby arrived. I checked its tiny form, wrapped it in a linen cloth, said a blessing for its long life, then handed the baby over to its proud mother. A fairy girl, fairy twins. What joy! This certainly was a night to remember. We were all smiling. A picture perfect family. Then the mother looked down, her belly again began to tremble. Another fairy baby? Surely not. I listened to her belly, paused, then held up three fingers. Three fairy babies would be born tonight. Another boy fairy followed another girl fairy. Quadruplets! Now, this *was* something special.

The night had been long and exhausting. I sat in a chair next to the bed, overjoyed and wishing I could rest and sleep. Then, right before my eyes, the family began to diffuse into a ball of soft light until they faded away altogether. The last thing to disappear from my view were the fluttering wings of the butterfly.

The next thing I knew, I was standing some way up the hairpin bend. I rubbed my eyes, shivered, and pulled my dressing gown tight around me. For a moment I wondered if I had been sleepwalking and dreamt it all.

With slow steady steps, I made my way back to my holiday cottage. Passing the shop with its trinkets in the window, the little pier, where boats jostled against each other in the lapping water, and up and down the steep braes where wildcats, sleeping now, were curled up in hollows of trees and long grasses.

When I opened the door to my cottage, the first thing I noticed was a steaming bowl of soup sitting on the table. It smelled so good. Even more curious, snaked around it lay an amber necklace that bore a striking resemblance to Granny's.

'Those fairies,' I said out loud. 'Blessings on you and your children, may you all live long and happy lives.'

Then, just as I was closing the door, something fluttered in and danced its way to settle on the edge of the soup bowl. I stepped up close and watched it unfold its wings. It was the unmistakable tracings of a tortoiseshell butterfly.

Well I never, I thought to myself, a huge smile spreading across my heart. I bent lower to get a better look. It appeared to look me in the eye, then throw its head back, as if in laughter. And I could swear I saw, within its tiny mouth, a tiny pair of loose-fitting dentures …

* A doula is a woman who gives support, help, and advice to another woman during pregnancy and during and after the birth.

10

THE WAGER

Imagine, if you will, a time back in the early 1300s, a time when Robert the Bruce was on Scotland's throne. It was early days in his reign and his rise to power had not been easy. There were fights and squabbles, certainly there was opposition. Not everyone agreed that he should be king, or have the power that he wielded. But despite all of this, he held fast, and sought any opportunity to promote and strengthen his position.

It was a time, too, of superstitions. Omens were always viewed as highly significant.

One day Robert the Bruce had been out hunting with a party of men in the Pentland Hills, when a white stag was spotted. This was cause for great excitement and the whole party set about chasing this rare and noble beast down.

For three days, men on horses thundered through the forest, dogs and falcons close at heel, in an attempt to flush out the poor creature. But it proved elusive and all attempts at tracking it down were unsuccessful.

The stag was of particular interest to Robert the Bruce because its capture would signify to all the people of Scotland that he was the true and rightful king. There was also a deeper connection: Robert the Bruce's great-great-great-great-grandfather, King David I, had, according to legend, come face-to-face with a charging white stag while out hunting. This had set off a chain of events that had ended with the building of Holyrood Abbey.

According to legend, when confronted by the white stag, fear stayed King David's hand and he held back from killing it. The stag had been cornered and charged at the king in desperation, aiming its set of deadly antlers right at him. But, in the final moment, it stopped stock still. It was in that bleak flash of a second that King David witnessed a sign of the cross illuminated between the stag's antlers. The moment the king looked the stag in the eye he vowed, there and then, to mark the occasion, for he felt that God had taken a hand in what had passed between them. True to his word, some years later Holyrood Abbey was completed, as testimony to King David's experience.

So, it was no surprise that Robert the Bruce thought the stag's appearance was significant. As a king, he too wanted the symbolism and luck that went with it. For him, the stag was to be caught at all costs.

The hunting party took a day to rest and were primed and ready to try again. The loyal noblemen were eager to please. The royal hounds were loosened and, having found the stag's scent, chased off into the Pentlands, the king and his retinue in hot pursuit. All day they hunted but caught only mere glimpses of the elusive stag, nothing more than that. The hunt was halted again and it was agreed that they would resume at daylight the next day.

The following morning, the hunting party reassembled. The king addressed them, calling upon each hunter to be vigilant, telling them that the stag must be captured.

'Is there anyone here,' he said, 'that will vouch for their dog's skills in bringing the stag down? A dog that can better the royal hounds who have so far failed in their task?' An uneasy silence fell as the party stood humbly before him. 'I will offer a reward, an incentive if you will …'

A shout came up from the back of the hunting party.

Among the ranks of noblemen were Sir Henry Sinclair and his young upstart son, William. The king held Sir Henry in high regard. He deemed him a trusted friend and loyal knight who had served him well, having fought at his side in several battles, proving his skills and prowess as a competent warrior. Sir Henry was an old hand at hunting but his son had very little experience to speak of.

William was yet to prove himself. Ruthless and hungry for recognition, his craving for status meant that he took unnecessary risks. His manner showed that he lacked the subtleties of diplomacy and courtly conduct. It was hoped that time and experience would 'knock the corners' off him, make him less cocky.

William jostled his way to the front of the party, causing horses to start and dogs to whine. Men muttered insults under their breath as he barrelled through on his horse. His two dogs – Help and Hold – led the dog pack, whipping between the horses' legs in an effort to stay at their master's side.

'Sire,' he cried. 'I'd wager ma twa dugs could bring that stag doon.'

The king peered at William's two deerhounds from the lofty height of his own horse. They were tall and slender, with broad heads and strong tapering muzzles. Their dark muscular frames were built for speed, and trembled with excitement and anticipation.

'Wager, you say?'

'Aye Sire, ma twa dugs – ma favourite dugs – Help and Hold here, they're the best dugs for miles around. They're fast, tireless and great hunters. If they canna bring the stag doon then none can. They'll kill the deer before it crosses the boundary at the March Burn. I'm sure of it.'

'I'll take your wager William. If your dogs are successful I will give you the forest of Pentland Moor, providing the dogs catch the deer within the boundary. But should they fail, I'll have your head.'

It was William who was trembling now. He dismounted his horse, and with shaky hands let loose his slow hounds first. Slow hounds were used to hunt and tire the stag. William paused to offer a prayer to St Katherine, then he mounted his horse and went after the stag, letting Help and Hold loose at just the right time.

The king stationed himself at the best vantage point to watch the chase. He glimpsed the stag, here and there, weaving through the forest. The dogs were gaining, far swifter than any of the royal hounds, their movements agile and fluid. The rest of the hunting party shouted encouragement but remained still.

Silence fell as they watched the stag, the dogs and William head perilously close to the March Burn boundary. When the stag bounded into the water, it seemed as though it had sensed this course could lead it to freedom. But the dogs had been gaining.

With incredible speed, Hold leapt into the water and managed to whip out in front of the stag, stopping its course and, for a split second, halting it altogether. Help played his part by driving the stag back onto the winning side of the stream. Then the two dogs worked together to bring the white stag down.

True to his word, the king granted William Sinclair the land he had promised in the wager. As for William, in gratitude for St Katherine's help, he built the chapel of St Katherine in the parish of Penicuik. To this day, the lands still remain in the hands of the Sinclair estate. And the rest, as they say, is history.

11

THE WHITE HARE

In the daurk furra o a rig
I saw an auld witch-hare this nicht
An she cockit a lissom lug
An luikit at the mune sae bricht
An she nibblit the green grouin.
An I wheeshit 'Shush, Carlin.'
Lik a ghostie ower rig loupit
Awa she, leavin mune shinin

Kindly translated by Donald Smith from Walter de la Mare's rendition of The White Hare

She stood among the hedgerows, engrossed with picking the brambles. Delicate fingers detached them from the bushes and dropped them into the basket she carried on her arm. From a distance she appeared to look like any of the other children in Temple village but when you moved closer something was not quite right.

It may have been the shape of her head, smaller than normal, or that small button nose

that had a nervous twitch to it. It was as though her face couldn't keep still. She was a fair-haired child, pale as milk and delicate, too. Her eyes were unusually round, rimmed red, giving way to luminous brown diminishing to blue, like melting pools. The rest of her frame was slight and all sinew. She fidgeted and was never one to seek or be seen in company, always at the hedgerows, picking and twitching.

She appeared in the village, out of nowhere, to live with her gran. She was just at that age where she didn't have to attend school – she was too old. Her grandmother, it seemed, had been in the village ever since it first started. Some used to say that she was the one that planted the seed for the old oak tree that stood at the edge of the village. Old Annie had shrunk with age, her back bent, and her rheumy eyes looked as though they saw something entirely different to everyone else.

When her granddaughter arrived she set about teaching her domestic duties and how to tend the garden, but kept her well away from the rest of the village and its gossips. Old Annie was wise enough to know that the eyes of the village would soon turn elsewhere. It was just the way things were, part and parcel of the usual rhythms of village life.

Now, it was a well-known fact that the men of the village, the farm labourers, saw it as their right to take from the land to help put food on the table. Some fished from the local stream or guddled trout, some set snares for pheasants or wood pigeons and others used their dogs for coursing – chasing rabbits and hares. Every little catch was added to the pot. Of course, we all knew that this was illegal. The laird never sanctioned this sort of thing; why would he? Anything to keep the tenants and labourers in their place. Occasionally, someone was caught and fined, to set an example to the rest of us. The activities would stop for a while but then, when harvests failed from too much rain or drought, or work was hard to come by, everyone did what they could to keep their families going.

One day, around about the same time that Annie's granddaughter arrived in the village, I was out with my father and some of his cronies. We had our dogs with us and had set out early across the fields with the intention of finding some rabbits 'for the pot' and also putting an end to a dispute about whose was the best dog. It was one of those hazy summer days. The heat was still in the ground and, as it rose, gave off a fuzzy moveable image. The smell of summer was caught in the breeze from the warmth of the earth, the sweetness of the haystacks, the green of the shady trees and the fruit and cobwebs of the hedgerows.

Our group stood about and talked a while, then stopped to follow my father's watchful gaze. His body spoke before he did, leaning forward, eyes narrowing, forehead furrowed. He spied something moving at the bottom of the field to the right. Without questioning, we let the dogs loose. They took off at high speed, covering ground in powerful bounds – the pack, neck and neck, heading straight for the boundary hedge. Soon they had flushed it out. A white hare.

Out it sprang, into the clearing, stopping momentarily to get its bearings. One of the dogs was a hair's breadth away from catching it. We all gasped out loud. Then, the creature zig-zagged across the field at lightning speed, long ears flattened against its head, legs stretched out moving fluidly, so fast the dogs were virtually left standing. We stood open-mouthed, watching it streak past us until it disappeared across another field to the side of old Annie's house and out of sight.

'A white hare,' my father gasped. He leaned on his tall stick and looked each of us in the eye. 'Do you know how lucky and rare they are?'

That evening the men talked of nothing else. Sitting by the fire in the pub, one of the men, old Jimmy, produced his lucky talisman from beneath his cap. It was a hare's foot. 'To ward off evil spirits,' he said. Bert stopped to light his pipe and, between puffing out plumes of smoke, began to tell us his story about seeing a black hare on the road one summer's eve and coming home to find his house on fire. More stories followed, tales of good and bad omens all featuring a hare or a rabbit. The more they talked, the more the hare became a prize to be had. It was agreed that another small hunting party would venture out the following weekend with the specific intention of catching the white hare.

It was a full moon that weekend, one that hung full and low in the sky, its belly an orangey-red as though it had been dipped in fire. A blood moon. Many pointed at it fixed in the sky and said in guarded tones that it was a bad omen or signified something bad was to come.

It had been decided that hunting the white hare would take place after the sun had gone down. 'The moon will provide enough light for what we need as well as cover from the laird's law enforcers,' laughed one of the men as he rubbed his hands with glee.

Seven of us set off, three dogs each, straining at their leashes. There was an air of excitement about the evening, an expectation despite the

foreboding moon. It took less than half an hour for the dogs to flush the hare out from its form. Away, across the fields it sprinted, flat out, swerving this way and that. Above the bats darted, black wings casting fleeting shadows, silent but for the crush of the cornstalks underfoot and the harsh breath of the chasing dogs. Only the blood moon bore witness, her light pooling across the landscape in a dim golden glow.

This time we were canny, we had some of the dogs positioned in various parts of the field in the hope that at least one would catch the hare. Again, just like the last time, it headed our way and sped past us in the direction of old Annie's house. Two of the dogs, lurchers Jed and Baz, the swiftest in the pack, tried to intercept its course, but it dodged them with the dogs snapping close at its heels and gaining.

Then, right before the high hedge in front of old Annie's house, just when it looked like the hare had nowhere else to run to, the hare paused, then, taking a giant leap, it cleared the 3m hedge. We watched in disbelief, sure that the hare's day was done. Its leap seemed to happen in slow motion, illuminated by the light of the moon, making it appear both silver and luminous. One of the dogs caught the hare's left hind leg and nipped it mid-air. Not enough to bring it down, but enough to hurt it as bloodstains were found on the dried grass in front of the hedge, at the point where the hare flew.

In an instant, we all ran along and around the hedge. We hoped that the wounded hare would still be there, and if not it would leave a telltale trail of blood on the other side of the hedge, which happened to be in old Annie's backyard.

It didn't take long before we found a thin line of blood spots. We followed the trail, which led right up to Annie's back door. A light was on in the kitchen and the back door was left ajar. I got to it first and, peeping through, I saw old Annie tending to her granddaughter, her long fair hair illuminated by the glow of the Tilley lamp. She looked pale and breathless, and her eyes had a startled look about them. For a moment, a split second, I thought I saw the outline of a hare sitting at old Annie's table but when I blinked, all I saw was old Annie with gnarled, arthritic hands, tending to her granddaughter's foot, her left foot, with a bandage.

Old Annie's granddaughter left the village not long after that and by strange coincidence so did the white hare, or so it seemed. The story of the white hare is still whispered on the lips of the locals today, particularly in the villages in and around Midlothian, but now it includes the idea that it now lives in the moon, for if you look carefully when next you see a full moon, you will see the outline of a hare.

Did you know: the brown hare is Britain's fastest land mammal, clocking speeds of up to 40mph.

12

THE HARPER'S STONE

It was a cold winter's night, the first night of the new year. Murdo MacMhuirich stepped out onto the freshly fallen snow, pulled his plaid tightly around him, then hitched his harp up onto his shoulder.

Murdo was a harper, a fine harper, the finest for miles around. His skills were called upon for all occasions: weddings, funerals and christenings. He attended gatherings to celebrate homecomings and played at ceilidhs both large and small. And on this night, he had been invited to sing and play his harp to welcome in the New Year at the laird's house, and was now on his way home.

Beyond, the woods were dusted with snow. As far as the eye could see there was nothing but a white hinterland. Murdo had quite the journey before him. On a good day, it would take him two hours on foot, but with snow and no track to follow the task would be much more difficult. Treacherous, even.

As he set off, the snow began to squall. He lent into the wind and put his best foot forward. He thought about arriving home to his wife, full with child. He thought about seeing his sons and daughters. He felt the weight of coins jingling in his pocket and smiled, confident in the knowledge that – thanks to the laird's generosity – there were enough funds to see the family through this cold spell, with perhaps extra for a few treats. His wife had her heart set on a new shawl, and how he would love to buy it for her.

He walked through the woods listening to the wind blowing through the trees, their creaks and groans as branches wavered under the weight of the snow, and the occasional crack as one gave way. In places, the drifts were more than 6ft high. Murdo had to navigate a path around them, slowing his progress. After a while he stopped to get his bearings. Looking around the wall of trees surrounding him, he realised he had strayed off the track, and was hopelessly lost. The cold was beginning to bite and his fingers, toes, even his nose, felt numb. Stamping his feet and patting his arms at his sides, he tried to bring back some feeling into his body.

Then he heard something. A noise from behind that sounded far off in the depths of the wood. It was the sound of something bounding over branches and snow. A deer perhaps? The sound increased. He stopped and looked back, and at first saw nothing but the glare of the snow contrasted with the blackness of the night. Barely breathing, he stood waiting, watching.

Then he saw them, the light of a pair of eyes, then another, and another. A sea of them, looking out at him from behind the trees. Fear coursed through Murdo's veins, rooting him to the spot. He couldn't think what to do. If he ran, they would chase him. Wolves loved to hunt. They were masters at it, and from what he could see there was a sizeable pack on his trail.

He cast his eye around for something that offered shelter, somewhere to retreat out of the wind and snow and provide safety from the wolves. Spying what looked like a large rock, he knew – if he kept his head – he might make it there even though it was some way off.

Walking swiftly, he headed towards the rock, all the while aware that the pack was gaining on him, getting closer. He could hear their panting and low guttural snarls. But the rock offered no shelter, nothing to crawl under or into. The wolves were virtually upon him, so he decided to grab a stout stick and climb to the top of it. At least from there the wolves couldn't all ambush him at once.

Once he had scrambled onto the top of the rock, he placed his harp down. The wind tore its cover off, carrying it away over the edge. He could see the pack had surrounded him. Its leader – an enormous black wolf – sat on his haunches and watched him with steely eyes. One by one the rest of the pack followed suit, sitting, watching. Then, lifting their throats to the moon, they howled. It was a mournful cry that echoed throughout the woods and into all the spaces in between.

Just as Murdo was wondering whether he would ever get to see his wife and family again, the wind blew and, catching the strings of the harp, it made them play. The wolves stopped howling and looked up at the rock.

At a loss to know what else to do, Murdo sat down and played his harp. The wolves quietened and lay down in the snow, listening to the

delicate notes. Some of them closed their eyes, lost in the beauty of the music. Murdo played on – but his hands and feet were frozen and his teeth began to chatter. So intent was he on continuing that he didn't notice the wolf pack leader spring up onto the rock behind him.

Something nudged Murdo's arm. He looked round to find he was face-to-face with the most enormous black wolf he had ever seen in his life. The wolf, however, wasn't threatening, it did not growl or snap. It did not show its sharp teeth. Its yellow fathomless eyes looked intensely into Murdo's without a hint of cruelty. Murdo was mesmerised, felt calm, even though he knew this creature could kill him outright.

The wolf moved closer and, lifting its great paw, held it up, whining as it did so.

Does he want me to look at his paw, thought Murdo, leaning forward and taking it in his hand. He peered closer, and embedded in a pad of the paw he found a jagged thorn.

With the utmost care, Murdo removed it. The wolf licked the wound with his great pink tongue, looked at Murdo as if to say 'thank you', turned his back, and with one great bound, leapt off the rock. He led the pack away off into the depths of the wood, leaving Murdo alone on top of the rock, thanking his lucky stars he was still alive.

The incident stayed with Murdo, and he told many of his friends and acquaintances about his brush with the wolves on top of the rock. The story was so often told that the stone itself became known as the Harper's Stone and is still referred to as such to this day.

It was some years later that Murdo happened to stop at an inn in Perthshire on his way back from playing at a wedding. He was sitting at a table having a bite to eat when a dark-haired stranger came and sat next to him, bringing Murdo a mug of ale. When Murdo looked up to thank him, he was struck by something familiar about the stranger, although he couldn't place what it was that made him feel that way. But when he looked into his eyes …

'Surely no?' Murdo barely whispered. The stranger smiled.

'Yes,' he said, nodding, then lifted his hand to show Murdo the deep scar on his palm between his middle and index finger.

The stranger spoke in a low soft tone. 'I was that wolf with the thorn in its paw. When you removed it, you lifted the enchantment that had been placed on me, and set me free. For that I cannot thank you enough.'

From that day on Murdo never feared travelling through the woods. Sometimes he felt the eyes of the wolves following him as he threaded his way through the trees and occasionally he would stop to play a gentle tune just as he did on that cold night when he played on the Harper's Stone.

13

THE GYPSY'S CURSE

This is a curious tale that involves a curse and the disappearance of all the birds from a certain estate in Ayrshire not so long ago.

Every morning, the laird inspected his estate. This morning was no different to any other: the laird had eaten, said goodbye to his young wife, mounted his horse and rode off to attend to his estate. It was a bright spring morning. As he looked across his fields, daffodils bobbed in the sunshine and labourers tended to the land with muddied hands and bent backs. Away in the woodlands, off to his left, crows cawed from their nests in the tops of the trees. It seemed all was well with the world and the estate. But then something caught the laird's eye. A fleeting colour of red moved in and out between the trees. It travelled slowly, steady but sure on foot. Occasionally the dappled sunlight framed the outline. The laird leaned forward in his saddle to get a better look, the leather saddle creaked as he did so. 'I thought as much,' he said, his thin lips taut across his wide mouth. Then he kicked on his horse with a little too much force. Startled, it snorted and made to bolt but the laird's cruel grip held the reins tight and sawed hard on its mouth. He cantered to the edge of the woodland.

From the shade of the big oak's canopies emerged an old gypsy woman. She was clad in an old shabby dress with a red shawl draped over her head and shoulders. On sight of the laird, she dropped a small curtsey, lowered her head and said, 'Good day to you kind, sir.' She knew it always paid to be polite when coming across gentry.

The laird, however, did not respond but looked down on her from the height of his horse. There was no warmth in his manner. He spat the words. 'And what do you think you are doing on my estate?'

'Kind, sir,' she said, slowly lifting her face to meet his glare, 'I'm on my way to the grand house over there. I have come to entice the kind lady who lives there to buy some of my wares,' she made to put her hand in the little wicker basket she was carrying.

'You shouldn't be on my land.'

'But, sir,' she protested softly as she remembered the last time she had visited the big house. She had been treated kindly, taken down to the kitchen and treated to a bowl of nourishing soup and a mug of ale before she left.

'Did you not hear what I said? Get off my land!'

'But, sir …'

'Do I have to repeat myself?'

Flustered, she dropped her trinkets back into her basket, covered them with a cloth and started off back down the path into the shade of the wood. But instead of returning the way she had come, she took a detour that took her off in a different direction.

When the laird looked back and saw her doing this he was seething. He turned his horse round and cantered up to where she was. As he approached, he raised his crop high in the air and brought it down once, twice, three times on the back of the old gypsy's shoulders. She let out a shrill scream, her knees buckled and she fell heavily on the floor.

'Now you will listen and do as I say won't you! Don't make me come back and do it a second time! Be off my land this instant.'

'I'll go, right enough sir,' she spat. 'And I'll be sure to take with me all the luck. I'll take all the crows and the magpies, and they in turn will take all the luck you ever had. You will have children, I promise you that. Aye, there will be plenty of lassies to keep the lovely lady of the house company, but for you, never an heir for the master. Your line will perish, you mark my words.'

And with that she got up off her knees, gathered her things and went off down the path that threaded through the woods and out through the gate that belonged to the estate. Shortly after, there was a great commotion high up in the treetops and as if in a great black cloud, all the crows and magpies lifted up, flew around the turrets of the grand house and then dispersed in different directions across the estate. After they had flown, the estate lands stood empty, devoid of any form of birdsong, or bird for that matter.

Over the years that followed the laird thought about his meeting with the old gypsy woman many, many times. His wife gave birth to three lovely daughters, which made her very happy and, as the gypsy had prophesied, kept her company. As for the laird, his wishes were never fulfilled. A son and heir to carry on the family line never appeared and so the house passed from uncle to nephew to cousin and on through six generations. Throughout all that time, never one of them produced an heir to pass on the family line. People talked, the labourers and tenants gossiped, the trees seemed to whisper words of the curse that was carried on the breeze. Throughout all that time, not a single bird was seen nor the slightest sound of birdsong ever heard. Even the beauty of the dawn chorus had disappeared, vanished into the oppressive gloom that cloaked the land.

Then, one day, a new laird arrived with his pretty young wife and he, just like the first laird, decided that he would ride out and inspect his estates. He happened to be travelling along the very same path that the first laird had taken when, who should he see making her way down through the woods, coming towards him, but an old gypsy woman wearing a red shawl. As soon as she was within 10 yards of him he doffed his hat and said, 'Good morning to you today my fine woman, and what do you have in your basket to delight us with?'

The old gypsy laid out the contents of her basket on the grass for the laird to see. They were nothing but worthless trinkets, certainly not fit for the likes of the lady of the house. The laird jumped down from his horse to examine the goods and picked out several bracelets fashioned from bits of tin and buttons. He put them in his pocket and in their stead he placed three gold coins. Then he said with a smile, 'Now then old woman, get yourself along to the kitchen at the back of the house and tell them I sent you and you are to have yourself a good meal before you leave the estate.' And with that, he climbed back on his horse and doffed his hat again, saying, 'A very good day to you,' and rode off into the bright sunlight. The old gypsy was dumbstruck.

A year and a day later the old gypsy woman found herself travelling through the estate once more. She was pleasantly surprised with the changes she saw around her. The people of the village were celebrating wildly. People were dancing and singing in the streets. Everyone greeted her with a smile and all around bunting and flags decked the trees and houses. She stopped to ask joyous passers-by what they were celebrating.

'Haven't you heard the good news?' they said. 'The laird up in the big house has had a son, an heir has been born, the first boy to be born in that house for over 100 years. The curse has been lifted.'

And as the old gypsy woman looked back at the laird's house, she noticed high up where the house flag fluttered in the breeze, crows and magpies circling around the big house's turrets and all among the tall trees of the wood. As she stood there, witnessing the celebrations, midst the shouts for joy and jubilation, the gentle sounds of birdsong lifted and carried on the air, and as soon as she heard it a smile played upon her lips. Luck had finally returned to the estate.

I first heard this story from the wonderful storyteller Audrey Parks, a gifted teller of tales.

14

THE SHETLAND WULVER

Many years ago there lived on the Shetland Isles a strange and elusive creature known as a wulver. Very few had seen it but there were many rumours of sightings. And so the stories grew so much that the boundaries of truth and fiction became blurred.

William had lived on the edge of the moor for an age now, louping over the bog cotton and grasses with ease as he made his way back and forth across the islands. His life had been solitary since his father died. William was 15 at the time. Up until then they had kept themselves to themselves out of necessity. William had tried to go to school when he was younger but had been teased because of the way he and his father looked. It hurt him to be called names or have the other children run away from him screaming, 'Wolfie! Wolfie!' You see, William was a wulver, which meant that he was unusually hairy. He also had fang-like eye teeth and he had a rolling gait to his walk. His unseen gifts were a heightened sense of hearing and smell; he could smell fear and sadness in equal measure.

He tried to fit in but after spending a whole year at school, despite all his efforts, he hadn't made one friend. In the end his father stopped taking him there and after that his night-time tears stopped.

His dad had been the one to introduce him to the stone at the loch. They had gone there late one night, wrapped in blankets against the cold with a thermos of hot chocolate and still-warm bacon sandwiches. There they sat under the stars marvelling at the Northern Lights. It was a magical night, sitting side by side with his dad, one of his happiest memories. Away in the distance they could hear the rousing shouts and cries of the island community celebrating Up Helly Aa.* He felt safe and happy away from the crowds.

When it rained, the stone became slippery. His father had warned him many a time, 'Steady son, or you'll take a fall.' But did he listen? No! One time he was in such a hurry he fell and cracked his head; he still had the scar to show for it just beneath his left eyebrow. He cried and bled so much they had to turn around and go straight home, not even stopping to catch fish. Sometimes, when he missed his dad, he would find his fingers reaching for the scar, as if it made him closer to him.

When the loch was calm and the night balmy, he would venture out. Prowling round the shores, he would look for a suitable location from which to fish, but his most favourite place was at the stone. It was large, smooth, and flat, the perfect size to accommodate his body and sometimes still held the heat of the day's sun.

He found guddling fish a far more relaxing pastime than fishing; hunkered over the stone, water up to his elbows, he waited until he felt the trout's subtle movement. His deft and delicate fingers tickled its belly like butterfly kisses, before wrenching it out of the water. It was a skill his father had taught him, like his father before him – a family tradition handed down through the generations.

He liked nothing better than to eat the fish there and then. If its size allowed, he would swallow it whole, head, tail, including the eyes. Sometimes he would swear he felt it still wriggling about inside. It made him want to jump up and down on the spot, shout at it to keep still and stop annoying him, but he hadn't quite got to that stage – yet.

William kept himself occupied. At sunrise he liked to watch the wild birds on the loch or go down to the seashore to count the seals. His dad was a practical man; he grew his own vegetables, kept chickens and goats and could fix virtually anything. But he was an old man even when William was young, so as he got older the burden of fixing the likes of the roof or cutting the peat fell on William, not that he minded. His dad was a good and patient teacher. Then one day his dad took a cold, or so he thought. A fever burned through his body and the cough racked him, leaving him gasping for breath. He insisted that he was fine but over the next few days visibly shrank beneath the bed covers. Then one day William woke to find his dad still and cold.

The years that followed were hard for William. He knew he was different. Deep down he sensed he didn't belong; he had nowhere to belong. He felt as though he was looking in at the world from the outside with no one to confide in. This was how he had always felt really, particularly now that his dad had died. He missed him terribly and still had so many questions to which he would never find the answers. He wondered about being a wulver, what did it mean and what was his purpose in life – surely not just survival? During that bleak time he took to roving about the islands.

It was the voice that drew him. It sang a soft lilting song that travelled out of an open window and was accompanied by the rhythmic sound of a shuttle moving back and forth across a loom. When he first spied her she was sitting with her back to the window, and her long red hair tumbled down her back and shone like the sun. It looked fierce and soft at the same time. He could relate to that. But it was the song that lured him, there was something about it that reminded him of … what? He couldn't quite put his finger on it.

The girl with the red hair at the window had certainly made an impression just by singing. William found himself travelling past the cottage more and more often. There was a loch nearby and he had convinced himself that it yielded the best trout. But really it was just a ruse, an excuse for him to catch a glimpse and hear her singing.

Sometimes he saw her walking the moor, her long red hair streaming out behind her. She would be collecting crottle found growing on the rocks that scattered the moorland. It was a natural dye for the wool she used for weaving. Her love of nature was obvious, he could tell. She would stand still and watch the skeins of geese flying south for the summer, hand shielding her eyes as they went. He had heard her laugh at the puddocks leapfrogging the burn and watched entranced as she danced around butterflies as their soft wings fluttered against the strong breeze. How he longed to approach her but fear of rejection and shyness held him back.

One early May morning he saw her walking across the moor, crottle-collecting basket in hand. On this occasion she took a different route to the norm, heading westward, away from the coastline. Although summer was on its way, there was still a mist cloaking the land. He watched her outline phase in and out, creating a ghostly figure. William felt uneasy, the hackles on the back of his neck had risen. Something was wrong, he could feel it in his bones, but he couldn't quite figure out what.

A sound pierced the morning quiet, like a dulled sob. At first he mistook it for the crow's cry but knew that crows didn't venture inland to the soulless moor. Turning his ear towards the direction of the sound, he stopped and waited.

The cry came once more. This time he could hear the anguish in its call and intuitively he knew something, someone, was in trouble. He began to run, his feet scrambling over the rocks and through brackish water, clods of mud flying as he moved swiftly, covering ground. Ahead he saw a movement, through the mist. The muffled cry came again.

When he got to where he thought the sound came from, he found the girl up to her neck in a peat bog. She had walked straight into it and was going under fast. There was no time to waste, William had to act quickly. Without thinking he grabbed her long locks and pulled.

It took what seemed an age to free her from the peat bog's lethal grip. They both lay panting on safe ground, covered from head to foot in black brown peat bog mud.

'Did you have to pull my hair so hard? It really hurt!' she said.

'Hmm, that's gratitude for you. I just saved your life.'

'And made me almost bald in the process.'

'Well excuse me!' William gave her a sidelong look and raised his eyebrows.

'Oh, I'm sorry. Can we start again?'

The two of them leant up on their elbows and extended their mud-stained hands for a handshake. 'Pleased to meet you, I'm William.'

'Martha.'

William was acutely aware of Martha's piercing gaze.

'Are ye for real?' she asked.

'How do you mean?'

'Well, you're certainly unusual to say the least.'

'Ahh, you're referring to my face … my umm …'

'Hair! You're what I'd call follically challenged. I'm not entirely sure you are human.'

'You're right, I'm not.'

'Go on with ye. You're having a laugh … aren't ye?'

William looked away, suddenly feeling acutely awkward.

'No. I'm serious.'

'Well, what are ye then? The Yeti of Shetland?'

William tipped his head back and laughed, his fangs exposed to the morning sky. He liked her frankness. It bordered on rudeness but he could tell that she wasn't meaning to be offensive. It made him feel accepted.

'I'm a wulver!'

'A what?'

'A sort of werewolf.'

'Oh no, don't tell me, you've saved me from the bog so ye can eat me? Just my flipping luck! By the way, I ate garlic last night so I might not digest too well.'

A giggle issued out of William's mouth. 'Oh do behave. I certainly couldn't eat you now I know you've been eating garlic.'

'And what are you doing out in the daytime? I thought werewolves only came out at night and howled a lot.'

'Stop it!'

They both giggled indulgently, then Martha's face changed. 'Oh goodness, I have to get back.' She jumped to her feet and started to run, calling behind her as she went, 'Bye, and thank yeeeeeeeeeee.'

William sat for a while, enjoying the stillness and savouring the smile that played on his lips. It suddenly struck him that Martha seemed totally unfazed by him being a wulver, she accepted him at face value. Well who'd have thought! Just as he was getting up he noticed something shining in the mud. He reached down and picked up a locket, and on it was engraved the name Martha. He ran back in the same direction, hoping to catch up with her but she was nowhere to be seen.

When he reached her house the door was slightly open and he tapped gently on the knocker. He could hear voices within, one slightly raised and sobbing, 'What are we going to do? I have no money for food now.'

Martha's voice followed, 'I can work the loom Mum,' she soothed. 'There's work to be had with that. Don't worry. We'll work it out, somehow.'

He tapped again. The voices stopped. Martha came to the door. 'Is everything alright?' said William. Her eyes looked to the floor as though searching for the answer, while tears spilled down her cheeks.

'You can tell me. I won't tell anyone. Besides, I don't have any friends to tell.'

Martha smiled and punched him softly on the arm. 'Idiot,' she laughed.

'Here, you forgot this,' said William, handing her the locket.

'Oh, thank you so much. I would have been devastated if I'd lost this. My dad gave it to me. Listen, you better go now, my mum needs me.' She closed the door quietly, leaving William to linger on the doorstep.

He moved on to the loch to wash. What he had heard had stirred something deep within him, it unsettled him. Picking up a stone, he threw it into the water and watched the ripples spread out and the fish dart beneath its surface. This was the place where he and his dad had spent hours skimming stones and watching the birds. It was his happy place. Together they had witnessed wading golden plovers stalking the loch's perimeter, red-throated divers flying low across its surface, and high up, soaring almost out of sight, a merlin. Once they spotted a rare greenshank and his dad got so excited he steamed up the binoculars, which made them laugh and frighten off the bird. But now William felt confused and a wave of sadness washed over him as he remembered his last moments with his dad. He felt helpless then as he did now. In his mind's eye he could hear his father saying, 'Just trust in the process son.' So he sat quiet, listening to the birdsong and trying to give himself up to the beauty of his surroundings and let go.

After a while, he sat up, dipped his hands into the water and, without thinking, caught a trout. 'Food. I'll take them food!' The thought of presenting them with fish, doing a good deed, made him feel happy and calm. It was his solution to their problem. Within no time, he caught another one. Later that afternoon, he left the trout on the windowsill of Martha's house, safe in the knowledge that she would notice it when she sat at the loom to work.

The following day he returned to do the same deed. Just as he put the fish on the windowsill, Martha popped up.

'I knew it was you, William. That is such a kind and thoughtful thing to do. Thank ye.'

'Think nothing of it. My pleasure,' said William, a wide smile appearing on his face.

'I'm going to collect crottle shortly. Would ye like to come?'

'I'd like that very much.'

William continued to leave fish in that manner until Martha's difficulties changed for the better. Their friendship blossomed and strengthened in the years to come, and the experience of gaining a friend and doing a good deed gave him a purpose. After that, William actively sought out others on the islands who were in a similar situation to Martha and helped by secretly providing fish for food. His calling card was by way of leaving the fish on their windowsill, just as he had done for Martha. Through these random acts of kindness the wulver reignited an old wulver legend on the Shetland Isles, one that still continues to this day – his stone is now named the Wulver's Stone and serves as a reminder of Shetland's wulvers.

* *Up Helly Aa is a tradition that originated in the 1880s. Since then the festival has been an annual occurrence in the Shetland calendar. Up Helly Aa is many things to many people and throughout the day there are experiences aplenty to be had by all from the celebration of Shetland history and the sight of the Guizer Jarl and his Jarl Squad marching through the town followed by his galley to the evening party in the halls.*

15

BETWEEN TIDES

It was long ago – in a time when stranger fish swam the tides, when huge creatures troubled the waters and the land was a shifting swamp. Our sea was a different hue then, denser, the current was stronger, it was occupied by more creatures – or so they say. On the banks lived the shell people, an altogether different type of being: noisy, given to volatile arguments, always bickering. In small groups they would assemble, crouching and foraging along the seashore, gathering shells that they cracked open with their sharp teeth, then swallowed quickly.

Although they sat on their haunches, they were never still for long. They were always anxious, alert. Mountains of spent shells, found strewn along the seashore, signified where they had been.

At times, the shell people hunted us with sharpened sticks. They would stand in the water up to their waists, their weapons held aloft.

Sometimes they were lucky. We learned to stay away – stay away from mounds of shells, the crouching, shifting groups. Away from their strong jaws, sharp teeth, and out of sight of their strange eyes.

Now, the story I am going to tell you dates back to that time – the time of defining, yes, that's what they called it. It all happened along this beach, here at Tentsmuir, Fife, and out there, on the shifting sand flats where our ancestors, and their ancestors before them, lay.

The story begins with one of our kind being speared by the shell people. He was the son of the King of Seals himself and, although wounded, he managed to escape. But in his frantic effort to get away from the shell people, he swam into forbidden waters and was caught by a fierce current. For some time he struggled against it, until it got the better of him and took him way up yonder, far from any place any of us had ever seen.

Eventually the sea spat him out onto a beach. Too weak to save himself – let alone fend off the circling birds – he made ready to meet his maker. Closing his eyes, he murmured prayers to the Great One, saddened that he would not be able to say farewell to his loved ones in the city beneath the waves.

Just at the moment when the prince was offering his final prayers, a young shell boy happened along the beach. He was altogether quieter, and sat less on his haunches, preferring instead to stand upright. There was something quite different about him in comparison to the other shell people. And when he came across the body of the wounded seal lying on the beach he was tender and set about cleaning his wound, feeding him and nursing him. He stayed there for days, never leaving the seal's side. The seal felt the breath of his life force growing stronger and stronger. After a time, the call of the sea drew him back, and at that point he knew he was ready to return – back to the city, his city beneath the waves.

His return was greeted with whoops of joy, and all the seals from far and wide came out to celebrate: barking and calling, slapping their flippers on the floor, rolling their great bodies in a joyous dance. Even the whales and the dolphins sent songs across the deep waters, like an echoing orchestra of love in sound.

But the story doesn't end there. From time to time the seal would venture back to the part of the beach where the shell boy had helped and healed him, and although he stayed in the sea, by putting his head up above the waves he would occasionally see the boy. Sometimes the boy would wave and let out a little cry, and sometimes the seal would answer by smacking the water with his flippers.

A year and a day passed, and the currents in the sea changed – fish stopped swimming in shoals and took off in all kinds of directions. It was as if they knew something big was going to happen. It was the same with the seals; they all claimed they could sense something was wrong, something was strange with their whiskers.

Instead of following their usual feeding routes, they stayed away from the sandbanks and headed for the city below where the waters were less turbulent.

And then it happened. The seawater began to run backwards in one big continuous wave, drawn back out into the ocean, gathering force, gathering momentum. There was still water in the city, of course, but much less of it, and all the fish disappeared completely.

Then a violent wind blew in, followed by wild lashing rains. Forked lightning lit up the sky, which turned dark, almost black. Out on land it was chaos. The sound of crashing, tearing and thudding was caught up in the fury of the wind, voices of distressed animals were snatched away. Trees uprooted and flew around, twisting in ever-decreasing circles. Spent shells, sand, rocks – everything it seemed – was caught up in torrential rain and wind coiling round and round, high into the air. Animals ran, heading inland away from the beach, the sea and the storm.

Then came an eerie silence, cold, frightening and still. Even the trees stopped rustling their leaves. Nothing could be heard, there was a

total absence of sound across the shore. Then, rising up like a huge angry wave, higher than the deepest parts of the sea, it came. Devouring all in its wake, rushing, rolling, roaring. Nothing was safe. It smothered the land, the trees, everything.

After a time, that seal, the king's son, put his head up through the surface of the seawater to watch events on the land. He looked to the beach – or where the beach used to be – and saw the body of a boy, carried on the crest of a wave. His friend, the shell boy. The king's son watched as the shell boy was thrown about like a rag doll. Without stopping to think, the seal swam towards the rolling mass …

The shell boy awoke in a pearlescent room to muted sounds of the sea surging back and forth like a constant sigh. His bed was made of soft seaweed. Anxious eyes looked on – round, watery, dark orbs – the eyes of several seals. The shell boy was too weak, too broken, to move. Giving himself up to his fate, he fell into a deep, all-encompassing sleep.

Days passed and he drifted in and out of consciousness. Soft muzzles and flippers fed him regurgitated fish and tended to his wounds. As the months passed, his body healed. But something strange had happened. Almost imperceptibly his body had changed, evolving to suit its surroundings.

Over the weeks he grew fur, a scale-like skin structure, his fingers webbed together, his body thickened and curved, and his eyes became similar to those of the seals.

When he returned to full health, the boy-seal remained with the seal community. He learned their ways: how to communicate, swim, eat, even how to sing. His integration with the seals was considered complete when he took himself a wife. Their union produced only one offspring. They pupped a beautiful girl.

She was brought up in the ways of the seals and to all intents and purposes looked like them, but, like her father, she could talk, and if you examined her closely, there within her flippers you could make out the vague shape of human hands.

As she grew older, the true extent of how different she was to the other seals became clear. At the time of the strongest tides, when the sea changed direction and the moon was at its fullest, she would leave the city and swim for a day and a night in search of land. So strong was her need, she overcame her fear of strange creatures that lurked in the murky sea waters. Once she arrived on land, a peculiar transformation took place. She would shed her skin and take human form.

And so the time of defining began. When she reached maturity, she took a mate. A handsome, strong seal from the community. And when they pupped, it was found that their offspring had also inherited her human traits.

This mix of part human, part seal was still part of us, the seal community. They looked very much like us but were altogether different. We were all aware of their 'call to land' and, over time, some of them ventured to mix with the folk that lived on the land. Sometimes they took a mate, sometimes they were forced to stay against their will. But they never stayed on land forever, always they found their way back home to the city beneath the waves. The sea always claims her own in the end.

And what did the humans make of us, I hear you ask? Oh, they had plenty to say all right. They called us selkies. We even adopted the term ourselves. Some humans thought we were the souls of folk lost at sea come back in a different form. Others said we were associated with the sidh, the wee folk. Most believed we were just a myth, stories made up to frighten children and old ladies. But they never learned the truth.

There was a time, a long while back, when I happened on to the land and stayed among human folk. This is a story I once overheard a young man tell at a ceilidh when called upon to tell a selkie tale:

My Uncle Jake, God bless him, he always swore he'd seen a selkie. Even went as far as saying one had saved his life. Course, my friends and I laughed at him, thought he was either having us on or had taken a wee bit too much of the drink. He liked his whisky, you see.

The story he told was always the same. He worked as a fisherman, up yonder where the Tay Road Bridge is now, but long before it was built – and aye, sometimes he would fish when he had had a drop too much of the whisky. He always claimed it kept the cold out. And like all fishermen in those times, he couldn't swim. Back then, most fisher folk believed that if the sea took you, it was your fate. You just accepted it.

And so it was one night, Jake was fishing, a little worse for wear from the drink, when the weather turned just as he was making his way back home. His boat got into difficulties and Jake was in no fit state to manage it. Waves began to swell, tossing the boat this way and that, until it overturned and he found himself struggling in cold, turbulent water.

As he felt himself sliding under, he knew the sea was about to claim him, and in his weakened struggle called out for help. Then something happened to change his fate. A seal came up underneath him, pushed him up out of the water so's he could catch his breath. They travelled like this for a while, Jake being propelled through the waves at some speed, until he was deposited on the beach.

Jake swore blind it was a selkie. Claimed he watched it emerge out of the water, lollop up the beach some way, and stop. Then to his sheer surprise, right there in front of him it shed its skin and transformed into a woman – the most beautiful woman he had ever seen. He said she was tall and lithe, that her skin shone bright in the moonlight, and her golden hair cascaded down her back. He was too weak, too exhausted, to say or do anything.

He claimed she lifted him up and carried him in her arms, back to his cottage. Now Jake was a mountain of a man, all muscle and gristle: he would have been even heavier in all that wet fishing gear, I should say. Anyhow, somehow she knew where he lived and what to do.

Inside Jake's cottage she busied herself with the range and brewed up some boiling water. Then he watched as she dropped a tiny shell into a pan. She told Jake that it would stop him getting a chest infection. Apparently the shell was a must for every selkie first-aid kit.

She stayed till early morning, singing him songs, and telling him stories of the sea and selkie life beneath the waves. He said she claimed that selkies originated from near here, from Tentsmuir. Jake said that, come the morning, just as the sun was rising, the selkie woman left, disappearing down the beach back to the sea.

He never saw her again.

Of course, none of us believed my Uncle Jake's story, we thought it was just that, one of his incredible sea stories. That is, not until after he died. Several of his family members, including me, his nephew, helped to clear his house. While going through his things we came across the shell. It was in amongst all his important papers, wrapped in tissue paper and kept in a wee box. He had kept that shell for years.

> It was a strange-looking thing, not like the usual shells you find on the beach here. We even took it to the museum to have it checked out, but no one could give us any information on it.

Everyone at the ceilidh listened to the young man intently. The story was received with rousing applause, and yet still among the listeners there were those who did not believe in selkies.

That's fine by me. It leaves the city beneath the waves and its population safe to carry on, as they have done for centuries.

But if you ever happen to come across a seal skin on the beach, I suggest you leave it be.

16

THE LAST OF SCOTLAND'S GIANTS

At the foot of a mountain was a wee town called Auchnaw. It was a quiet, orderly place, where everyone went about their business quite happily until the day a giant moved into the area.

The giant lifted up his big nose and sniffed the air. 'Oooooh,' he chuckled. 'Whit's that I smell? Mebbe a puckle o' bairns.' He clapped his big chubby hands together with glee startling some grouse hiding in the long grass. 'I think I'll tak a wee daunder doon the ben.' And off he went, his big feet flattening grass and crushing rocks as he followed his nose, sniffing with great intakes of breath, down the mountainside.

'I'm jist in the mood fur some bairn-pie,' he said, stopping to pat his rather large round belly. He looked about him, shielding his eyes with a pudgy hand. 'Where are yoos ma wee bairns?' he sang in a playful voice. 'Come oot, come oot wherever yoos are.' Moments passed, even the birds in the trees held their breath. His roguish smile dropped. No child came out. He straightened himself up and made his big hands turn into fists. In a low whisper he hissed, 'Mind I can smell yoos – an if I can smell yoos, I can find yoos.' From somewhere nearby a small muffled wail issued. Beyond, in a set of rocks not 50 yards away, a frightened group of children huddled.

'Och aye! So we want tae play games do we?' The giant moved, deliberately stomping, making the ground shake, his laugh cruel and teasing as he did so.

'So, let me see.' He picked up a tree, totally uprooting it. 'Am I gettin warmer?' He upturned the tree and gave it a thorough shoogle. 'Are yoos in here?' Nothing fell out and so he tossed it over his shoulder.

Next he moved on to a little wooden bothy. 'Aye, I bet yoos are in here. Are yoos?' He picked up the bothy between his thumb and forefinger, took a keek inside, then lifted it to his nose. While inhaling deeply, its door became detached from the house and then wedged up one of his nostrils. The giant was taken by surprise. 'Oooh, nasty wee hoose. Noo I've got something up ma neb!' He then dropped the bothy on the spot and shoved a stubby finger up his nose. For several minutes he hoaked about. Finally he removed his finger, complete with bothy door and rather a large dollop of bogie. 'Ah, got-ye!' he said as he peered at the broken and splintered bogey-covered door before putting it promptly into his mouth. 'Whit is fur ye, wull no go by ye!' and swallowed it down with a gulp.

Then he paused, mouth open, eyes watering from a sneeze making ready to explode. 'Aaaaaaaatchooooooooooooooo!' The gust of wind he created sent some birds who were flying up ahead off course, while at the same time a stream of snot shot out and pinioned a poor rabbit to a rock. The giant wiped his nose with the back of his hand. 'Hmmm, sneeze on Monday, sneeze fur danger. Weel,' he chuckled again, 'that's about richt fur the wee bairns hiding behind here.' Suddenly he pounced, nimble fashion for a 10-ton giant, and picked up a large rock. The children hiding behind it scattered in all directions. He raised his fist and attempted to swat them, thumping the ground this way and that, but they were too quick for him, all except for one.

Tilly, the youngest and smallest of the children, was frozen to the spot with fear. She had crawled to another rock nearby. Her sobs drew the giant's attention. 'Oooh, whit's this I can hear? A bairn havin a wee greet?' He stopped to cup a hand over his ear. 'I can hear ma breakfast.' He made to walk over to where Tilly was hiding and he was just about to bend down and find her when ... THWACK! A rock stung him hard on his bottom. The giant clumsily burled around. 'Och, that wis ma bahookie! Who did that?' he demanded, rubbing the sore spot.

Another missile flew through the air and hit him on the ear. 'Aaooww,' shouted the giant. 'That wis ma lug!' Meanwhile, another child rushed in behind him, scooped Tilly up in his arms and whisked her away. Then another missile sailed into the giant's path and smacked him squarely on his nose. 'Och, that wis ma neb! Stop that the noo or I'm gonnae go raj!' A wee boy suddenly showed himself 300 yards away down the mountainside.

'Tumshee-muckle-heid, we all wish that ye wiz deid!' he taunted, then he turned round and wiggled his bahookie at the giant. Another child appeared much further off to the left and shouted. 'Over here muckle-heid!' Soon a chorus of voices were chanting and hollering, and children started popping up all over the mountainside. The giant became visibly annoyed. 'Haud yer wheesht!' he bellowed, covering his ears with his hands. He got easily riled and it showed. His face swelled up, flushing several shades of red, and he stamped his feet, dislodging rocks and sending them tumbling down the mountain. With bulging eyes and flaring nostrils he shouted. 'Yooooooooooo nasty wee bairns. Ye's are daein ma heid in ...' Then he turned and picked up the nearest rock and hurled it at the first child he saw, followed by a volley of more rocks that went bouncing down the mountainside and veering perilously near the town. The children took to their heels and sprinted as fast as they could, squealing as large rocks bounced past them.

With all the commotion, concerned parents came dashing out of their houses to gather up the children and take them to safety.

The giant, his burst of anger over, sat himself down on the mountainside breathing heavily. 'I dinnae like they sleekit bairns. I'm gonnae huv tae eat *all* o' them! Then they'll no bother us ivver agin wull they?' He nodded his head, agreeing with himself.

Meanwhile, all the townsfolk gathered in the community hall. The town councillor, Mrs McMooney, had taken to a small platform before them. 'Friends, the time has come. We cannae live wi' this threat tae our bairns, our safety, our livelihoods. It's no right. We have tae come up wi' a plan. Does anyone have ony suggestions?'

'Aye, I do,' said Maggie Wishart, the town librarian. 'We could try poisoning him.' Around her, voices muttered in agreement.

'But whit wid we use for poison and just exactly how much wid we need?' asked Dorothy, the local bee keeper.

'And whit if it poisoned us while making it?' piped up old Euphemia McKinnon. More voices muttered in agreement.

'It's too dangerous. Whit aboot another idea?' said the councillor.

Everyone looked about as though deep in thought, trying to think up another good idea. You could have cut the atmosphere with a knife.

People began drooping their shoulders and hanging their heads. Mothers gathered their children up and held them close. 'Whit are we gonnae dae?' one of them cried.

Tilly then emerged from the crowd and climbed up on to the platform. 'Can we no dig a great muckle pit and lure the giant intae it?' A murmur began to rise in the room. Tilly went on, 'When we had oor last firework nicht the giant stayed well awa. I think he disnae like fire and loud bangs, unless he maks the bangs himsel. I think he's feart.'

'I think she has a point,' agreed the councillor.

'We'll no ken unless we try it,' piped up Malcolm McManic, the local mechanic.

'Dig a pit!' cried Lynn Hill, the town's garden designer.

'Dig a pit!' chorused the rest.

'I've a good selection of shovels,' said Mr Creosote, the church grave digger.

'That's settled then,' pronounced the councillor, and before the sun rose the next morning all the folk had dug their pit and made a plan.

The pit was deep and at the bottom was a heap of brittle, flammable wood and materials doused in a special mixture, made by Mr Creosote. It was guaranteed to create a roaring fire.

Older children and their dads were given the task of luring the giant down the mountainside to the waiting pit covered over by chopped-down tree branches. Overnight there had been much activity, with the mums making giant sweeties, the infamous Auchnaw tablet. It's a well-known fact that giants have a very sweet tooth and so the tablet was the obvious choice.

A trail of Auchnaw tablet was laid from the mouth of the cave where the giant lived, leading down the mountainside. At a certain point, 200 yards from the pit, two of the dads were to tease the giant with some tablet and a lot of name-calling, make him mad enough to want to chase them – and get hold of the tablet, too.

The plan worked like clockwork. The giant's sense of smell drew him out of the cave and directly to the waiting sweeties. He followed the trail, like Hansel and Gretel's trail of white pebbles. When the dads appeared, they created a stooshie, taunting him with sweeties and name-calling. The giant was raging, fit to burst, and chased the dads right up to the pit and, crraaaaaaash, down he fell.

Mr Creosote acted quickly, he threw the burning sticks down into the pit where the primed kindling ignited with a whoosh. The families and their children danced, and all the townsfolk danced. A band of pipers struck up a rousing reel and the fire in the pit burned brightly. Soon all of the pit was ablaze, the flames flickered and leapt as the dancers burled and skirled to lively tunes. There was an enormous sense of joy about the place. The giant was dead and now they all could live in peace … or could they?

As the fire burned down, people began to notice small cinders and ashes rising into the air, and gathering into what looked like a black cloud. The cloud seemed to move of its own accord, hovering over all the people. Then, quite abruptly, it dispersed. When it did so, everyone started to slap their arms, their heads, their legs, dancing on the spot and gyrating in an altogether odd fashion while they yelled and squealed, itching like mad all over. The cloud, as it turned out, was made up of hundreds and thousands of teeny tiny biting creatures.

Since then they have become known all over Scotland, but particularly throughout the west, as 'midgies'. Indestructible, detestable and very, very annoying little creatures.

And that is the story of how midgies came to be.

17

KING OF THE BIRDS

'If you settle down now and keep quiet, I will tell you exactly how things were.' The chicks cooried down in their nest, huddling together to keep warm, feather against feather, their wee claws folded beneath each tiny body. Their mother, a blackbird, cocked her head sideways and began her story.

'There was once a time when all the birds were just birds. There was no pecking order, no competition, no getting in a flap over silly things. We accepted each other for who and what we were, no matter what size or colour of feather. No matter how sharp the beak or claw. Flight was something we just did or didn't do. The emphasis was on who you were, your unique individuality, that's all.

'But then, one day, something changed. I couldn't quite tell you what happened to cause this but all of a sudden all the birds started squabbling. They began by throwing insulting tweets at each other, comparing one bird's flight to the others, claiming that certain areas of the sky belonged to certain species or individuals and not others. Trying to fly anywhere without upsetting anyone became a nightmare. Talk about a pecking order, there simply wasn't any order at all. Your grandma told me she had sleepless nights over it, so much so that she got in a muddle and started to wake before the dawn. She became so stressed and anxious that some of her feathers fell out too. Grandpa said her tweet turned into a peep. "She simply went out of tune," was what he said.'

'So Mum, tell me, how did it get sorted?' asked one of the chicks.

'All the birds were getting their feathers in a twist. It got to the stage that hardly anyone was bothering with the dawn chorus. Migrations weren't happening, which was having a disastrous effect on certain bird populations, quite gravely I might add. And then there was the problem with birds not being in their right place at the right time – it was affecting other species of animals. This in turn resulted in other ecosystems getting upset. Everything was getting out of control and no one knew who to blame.'

'That's awful. So what happened to create a change?' asked another wee chick.

'Well, some of the birds got together and decided to call a meeting.'

'Which birds, Mum?' the chicks chorused.

'Birds like owl, swallow, thrush, robin, blackbird and even golden eagle came back from soaring over lochs and mountains to take part. All the usual ones and more besides.

'After a lot of tweeting and twittering and everyone talking at once, peacock got everyone's attention by trumpeting its alarm call. Apparently it's very loud! Some of the birds were nominated to sit on the bird council, I forget which ones now, but it didn't include our bird-brained cousins like the Dodo.'

'Aren't they extinct, Mum?' quizzed the largest chick.

'Ah yes, well, that would account for why they weren't there! Anyway, following a long debate it was decided that the bird kingdom needed a king.'

'A king?' all the chicks gaped, their wee beaks wide open.

'Yes, someone in charge to make decisions.'

'So, how was that decided?' asked one of them, emerging out of a broken egg.

'With a contest.'

'What type?' asked another chick.

'One to see who could fly the highest. So, all the birds assembled. They went up in flocks of fifty to start, with a representative from each species in each flock. Of course, there were quite a few ruffled feathers and pointing of beaks. The penguins weren't impressed, said the contest was fixed because they couldn't join in on account of not being able to fly. Well, that started everyone off about what constitutes a bird and all "real" birds should fly. So silly, and the poor penguins, emus and ostriches really got their beaks put out. But, like owl said, you can't make an omelette without breaking eggs. Some things had to be said and aired.

'Anyhow, the competition started. It soon became clear that some birds were just better equipped than others. The heavier birds, like the chickens and turkeys, flapped about a lot but hardly made it off the ground. Grandma had to stuff grit in her beak to stop herself laughing out loud, but sshhh don't tell anyone.

'And then there was the likes of the song birds. Yes, they could get themselves up in the air but at a certain height they got buffeted about by the wind and didn't stand a chance of getting anywhere up to the thermals. The vultures and hawks did well mind.

'But, as expected, the strongest of the golden eagles climbed higher and higher up into the sky with all the other birds falling back one by one. Grandma worried that some of the less able ones would fall into the sea or get lost on one of the islands. From the ground below they all craned their necks trying to pick out the golden eagle's speck in the sky.

'Golden eagle got a bit full of himself when he saw the last of the birds peel away and head earthwards. It had been quite an effort for him and he was feeling quite pooped and was just starting his descent when he heard a wee voice to the side of him tweeting, "I am King, I am King!" When he looked he saw a wee brown wren fluttering above him.'

'But Mum, how could a little wren fly so far up?'

'Good question son. She was clever. She had hidden among his feathers seated on his back as he flew up into the sky.'

'She's no daft is she?'

'No, but there was a price to pay. When she got down all the little birds were delighted as they were sure that the bigger birds would win but didn't dare tweet up and complain. The bigger birds were furious, claiming that the wren had cheated and it was unfair.'

'Really? Mum, it wasn't fair though was it?'

'No, but was the competition fair in the first place? Anyway, they decided to hold a new competition. Only this time based on which bird could swoop the lowest. The competition began and guess what?'

'What?'

'The wee wren saw a wee field mouse hole and climbed into it, singing, "I'm King, I'm King!" Well, the large birds were outraged. Grandad said he thought the peregrine falcon was going to have a canary!'

'Oooh, did she?' they all chorused, with beady eyes on Mum.

'No she didn't! Anyway, they stood over the hole for hours vowing to ruffle the wren's feathers when she got out.'

'And did they catch her, Mum?'

'No son, even to this day she still claims to be king, even though really she should be called queen, because, after all, she is a female bird.'

'But I've never seen her – ever.'

'That's because the little brown wren is feared of all the big birds out there that are still cross with her. So she stays well hidden among the hedges and bushes. But if ever you need advice, she is always available, you just need to know where to look. Now, close your eyes and go to sleep. I don't want to hear another peep out of you.'

GLOSSARY

ah	I
about	about
aye	yes
awa	away
bahookie	bum
bairns	children
breikfast	breakfast
cannae	can’t
daein ma dinger in	doing my head in
dauner	walk
deid	dead
doon	down
fer	for
feart	afraid
gonnae	going to
greet	cry
haud yer wheesht	sshh/be quiet
heid	head
hissel	himself
hoose	house
hoaked	raked

huv	have
intae	into
keek	look
ken	know
lug	ear
neb	nose
nicht	night
noo	now
ma	my
mebbe	maybe
muckle	big
oot	out
puckle	a few or handful
raj	mad
richt	right
sair	sore
shoogle	shake
sleekit	sly
stooshie	commotion
tae	to
yoos	you
ye	you
wee	small
whit	what
wid	would

The Scottish Storytelling Centre is delighted to be associated with the *Folk Tales* series developed by The History Press. Its talented storytellers continue the Scottish tradition, revealing the regional riches of Scotland in these volumes. These include the different environments, languages and cultures encompassed in our big wee country. The Scottish Storytelling Centre provides a base and communications point for the national storytelling network, along with national networks for Traditional Music and Song and Traditions of Dance, all under the umbrella of TRACS (Traditional Arts and Culture Scotland). See www.scottishstorytellingcentre.co.uk for further information. The Traditional Arts community of Scotland is also delighted to be working with all the nations and regions of Great Britain and Ireland through the *Folk Tales* series.

Donald Smith
Director, Tracs
Traditional Arts and Culture Scotland